Filthy Coach

Filthy, Volume 7

Amy Brent

Published by Amy Brent, 2021.

FILTHY COACH

First edition. April 7, 2021.

ISBN: 979-8201631536

Written by Amy Brent.

Also by Amy Brent

Filthy
Filthy Boss
Filthy Doctor
Filthy Professor
Filthy Seal
Filthy Cowboy
Filthy Daddy
Filthy Coach

Forbidded
The Doctor's Fake Marriage

Forbidden
Fake Fiance
One More Chance
Crave Me
My Best Friend's Dad
The Doctor's Fake Marriage
Dad's Best Friend

Forbidden Fantasies
Daddy's Business Partner
Daddy's Friend
Daddy O
Climbing His Corporate Ladder
Taken By Daddy's Boss
Filthy Liar

Standalone
Teachers' Pet
Filthy Box Set
Knocked Up By My Brother's Best Friend
My Best Friend's Brother
My Best Friend's Ex
Say You're Mine
Club Desire Box Set
My Boyfriend's Dad
Fighting For Her
Forbidden Love Box Set
Love Undercover
Friends With Benefits
A Royal Menage
Baby Fever
Vegas Baby
Brother's Best Friend for Christmas
Christmas With My Best Friend's Dad
My Son's Sitter
Single Dad's Christmas Present
Surrendering To 3 Alphas

Because I Love You
Catching Up With Daddy
Claiming Cinderella
Double Trouble
First Love
First Time
Knocked Up By My Brother's Best Friend
My Best Friend's Boyfriend
Pretend Daddy
Redemption
Roomies With Benefits
Royally Yours
Rub Me The Right Way
Show Stopper
That One Night
The Baby Contract
Truth Or Dare
Santa's Naughty List
Quickie on Christmas
Con Man

Table of Contents

FILTHY COACH
by
Amy Brent

This is a work of fiction. While, as in all fiction, the literary perceptions and insights are based on life experiences and conclusions drawn from research, all names, characters, places and specific instances are products of the author's imagination and used fictitiously. No actual reference to any real person, living or dead, is intended or inferred.

What do you do when the sexiest bastard to walk on to football field happens to need your personal services?

Sam Carson is a washed-up ex-quarterback who's more famous for his drunken brawls and internet sex tapes than throwing touchdowns. So why did my father, the owner of the Atlanta Trojans, hire Sam to be the new head coach? And what part does he expect me to play in this dangerous game?

ALLIE WINSTON: I'm a tough chick playing in a tough man's game. I'm a sports image consultant. It's my job to make undisciplined football players and unfriendly coaches heroes in the public eye. But when I'm assigned to make Sam Carson look good, I know that I have my work cut out for me. Especially when he catches me in the shower diddling myself and moaning his name. I can't deny my feelings for Sam, but I can't deny that I'm also part of a game that's using Sam as a pawn. I can only hope that he never discovers my treachery, because I can't imagine my life without Sam in my bed.

SAM CARSON: I'll be the first to admit it. I'm a baaaad boy. I drink hard, play hard, and screw hard. And when I drive my Lambo into the back of a truck, my career as one of the hottest quarterbacks in pro football comes to an end. For the last few years I've been a coach. When I get an offer to be the head coach of the Atlanta Trojans, I know something is fishy. Then I meet Allie Winston, the smoking hot daughter of the team owner. I want her and I know she wants me, but I get the feeling that there's more than just sexual attraction at play. Allie seems to be playing a dangerous game, and I won't stop until I find out exactly what – and who - is going down.

CHAPTER ONE: Sam Carson

People often ask me, Sam, what's the best part about being famous? They assume it's having tons of money in the bank or a fleet of exotic cars in the driveway of your fifty-room mansion, or the adoration of millions of fans that makes a star's toes tingle.

Bullshit.

My favorite part about being famous, if you can even call me that anymore, is the groupies: those wonderfully-slutty ladies of questionable judgment who will suck your cock beneath the table in a packed nightclub or fuck you silly in a stall in a football stadium restroom during halftime.

Groupies come in all ages and colors, all shapes and sizes, all willing to take it however you wanna give it to them. In the mouth, the pussy, the ass; whatever.

It's all the same to them and all the same to me.

There's one thing you must understand about groupies. It actually has nothing to do with you; at least not the *real* you. It's all about the *famous* you; the *you* the public thinks they know; the *you* they see on TV or in magazines.

And they're not fucking or sucking the famous you for sexual satisfaction, but for bragging rights; so they can they can brag to their groupie friends, "Hey, I fucked him! Let me tell you all about it!"

Think about it, how many women can honestly say they fucked an American Football League quarterback in the equipment closet during halftime of a national championship playoff game?

Just one that I know of.

And I only know that because I was the one doing the fucking.

I don't remember her name, but she'll take those bragging rights to her grave. Most people won't believe her when she tells the story, but that's okay because she knows in her heart that it's true.

When you're famous, regardless of the reason why, groupies are a part of the game.

Mick Jagger has a line of hot twenty-year-old's five miles long ready to fuck him, even though he is older than the Crypt Keeper and looks like he's decomposing before our eyes.

Singers, actors, athletes, billionaires all have their groupies.

Even psycho killers have women ready, willing, and able to have sex with them.

Charles Manson still gets love letters from women who want to bear his lovechild, even though he's been locked in prison for serial murder for forty-four years.

Both of the Menendez brothers got married *after* they went to prison for shot gunning their parents to death.

Fucking OJ Simpson got more pussy after he killed his wife and her friend than ever before.

Groupies can't control themselves.

That's part of the allure and part of the danger.

They're like bloodhounds.

They can sniff you out wherever you go, always on the lookout for a famous name to tug, suck or fuck, so they can post it on Facebook or brag to their equally-slutty girlfriends about who they had in some hole of their body.

Hell, you didn't really have to that big of a star to have groupies attracted to you like bees to honey. Or flys to shit.

Just look at me.

I'm a good-looking guy, but I'm not super rich – at least not anymore – and I'm more famous for who I used to be than who I am now.

Side note: I have noticed an increase in age and a degradation of hotness of the groupies who approach me now.

Maybe that's it.

The quality of the groupie declines in direct proportion to the decline in the level of fame.

When you're Sammy Carson, the starting quarterback of a nationally-ranked college football team, or Sam Carson, the franchise quarterback of an AFL team that plays on TV every other Sunday night, the quality of groupie is incredibly high.

But when you're Sam Carson, the former quarterback whose throwing arm got mangled in a car wreck, virtually ending your playing career overnight, and you have to go into coaching just to keep a foot in the game, the groupies slip from 10's or 12's down to 7's or 8's.

I'm not complaining.

Even 7's and 8's rank a hell of a lot hotter than most normal guys could ever hope to get.

They wallow in pussy belonging to 4's and 5's, and they're happy to get it.

In professional sports, groupies are everywhere.

And they play at every level of the game of football.

When I was the starting quarterback of the Nassau College Buccaneers, the cheerleaders used to line up outside the locker room, waiting to see which one I'd pick to spend the night with.

Some nights, I'd take two or three of them home with me, which pissed off the rest of the team because they got my leftovers.

Sorry, fellas. Maybe you can get a majorette to blow you on the bus ride home. If not, you can work your way through the bevy of female alumni who would love to get a young buck in the sack.

I'm the star. I get first pick. Fuck you very much!

When I was drafted into the pros as the backup quarterback for the New York Thunder, women came out of the woodwork like cockroaches to be with me.

When I became the team's franchise quarterback, I was with a different woman every night, on and off the road. I'd have to take a day off every now and then just to give my poor cock a rest.

Even now, as the forty-two-year-old head coach for the Atlanta Trojans, the groupies still come on to me.

"Say, didn't you use to be Sam Carson, the quarterback of the New York Thunder?" they ask all wide-eyed and giggly.

"Why yes, I did," I politely reply. "Would you like my cock in your mouth or in your twat?"

That's pretty much how the conversation went when I pulled off Interstate 16 coming out of Atlanta to take a piss and refuel my Land Rover on the way to my boss' beach house in Hilton Head, South Carolina.

The girl behind the counter, a smoky-voiced gal around thirty-five or so, with red-dye hair and big tits, spotted me right away.

"Hey, ain't you Sam Carson?"

I smiled and bobbed my head. "I am."

"I'm Janine," she said in a thick southern accent. She rolled her tongue around her plump lips. "I just love the Atlanta Trojans. I bet you'll look so handsome down there on the sidelines with your little headset on."

"Let's hope so," I said with a sigh, nodding toward the gas pumps. "I also had thirty-five in gas."

I set the two six packs of Coors on the counter and held out my credit card so she could ring me up. She didn't reach for the card. Instead, her eyes went dreamy and she pursed her lips.

Bingo.

Groupie alert.

I stuck the credit card back in my wallet and gave her a smile. "So, do you want me to sign your tits or something?"

That was all it took. She came around the counter without another word. She brushed past me to lock the front door, then led me into the back room.

I bent her over a stack of beer cases and gave it to her from behind.

Hers was not the tightest twat I'd ever stuck it in, but it did the trick.

Ten minutes later, I was back on the road with a full tank of gas and two six packs of Coors; all on the house.

See.

What'd I tell you.

Groupies.

They are fucking awesome.

CHAPTER TWO: Allie Winston

It took nearly five hours of driving in heavy interstate traffic to get from my loft in downtown Atlanta to my dad's beach house on Hilton Head Island, just off the coast of South Carolina.

It was slow going, but I enjoyed the peace and quiet of the long drive. I looked forward to the solitude of a long weekend at the beach. It was Friday afternoon and I wasn't due back in the office until Tuesday.

I planned to spend the entire weekend alone with several bottles of my dad's best Chardonnay and the latest John Grisham novel.

I wasn't even taking a computer with me.

It would be the first time I'd been off the grid in years.

Okay, I wouldn't be totally off the grid. I had my iPhone, but you can't expect a girl to go cold turkey all at once.

I promised myself that I would not surf the web or answer any calls that weren't from my dad or Darcy, my assistant back in Atlanta.

Darcy would text 911 if anything caught fire at the office and would only text if it was a raging inferno that she couldn't put out.

And dad, who owned the Atlanta Trojans professional football team, was in Los Angeles at a team owner's meeting, so I didn't expect to hear from him until later next week.

Honestly, if I didn't see, speak, or hear from another human over the next three days, that would be just fine with me.

Once I got out of the horror that is Atlanta traffic and hit Interstate 16 east, I set the Audi's cruise control to sixty-five, plugged in the latest Bruno Mars CD, and sang along at the top of my lungs. I felt great, like I was leaving the world and all its troubles behind, at least for a few days.

I drove with my shoes off and the windows down. I loved the feeling of the wind caressing my cheeks and whipping through my long blond hair.

It was springtime in Georgia. The air was warm and moist, but the breeze was cool and refreshing the closer to the ocean I came. I glanced out the side windows and gave a happy sigh.

The world had turned green again after a dull winter that left me greatly in need of a break.

I call it a break rather than a vacation because if I don't get away once in a while to decompress, I'm liable to break things over people's heads.

I handle stress pretty well, but every now and then it gets to me. I work as a public relations and image consultant for one of the top sports marketing firms in the country, based in Atlanta.

I work mostly with professional athletes playing in the southeast, including those who play for my dad's team, the Atlanta Trojans.

It's a stressful job, but I love it and can't imagine doing anything else.

I get to work with my father without having to work directly for him. He's my client, not my boss. I wouldn't have it any other way. I love him dearly, but I could never work for him.

Daddy can be a bit of a bully, which he says you have to be if you're going to make it big in the cutthroat world of professional sports.

Daddy doesn't stress me out, at least not since I've become an adult who has proven that I can take care of myself.

My stress typically comes from my personal life; mostly from the long line of random assholes who worm their way into my bed and into my heart, then turn out to be total douchebags who are either (a) afraid of commitment, (b) already involved with someone, but forgot to tell me about it, (c) convicted felons on the run from the police, (d) gay, but experimenting with women, or (e) all of the above.

You think I'm joking.

Trust me, I'm not.

The latest douchebag to tromp through my life was Brett, the hot-as-hell younger brother of a (now former) friend who couldn't wait to meet me, fuck me, steal my debit card, and clean out my checking account.

The joke was ultimately on him. My bank automatically sweeps everything over a set amount into my money market account, so good old Brett just got away with a hundred dollars and my everlasting contempt.

I wouldn't have minded the robbery so much if the sex had been better.

I guess I should add another option: (f) sucks in bed.

Newborn babies could hold erections longer than Brett.

Turns out, too much cocaine will do that to you.

There's even a name for it.

Coke dick.

Who knew?

I pushed thoughts of Brett's worthless ass out of my mind as I turned onto Interstate 278. I was less than thirty minutes from the house overlooking a private sandy beach on the ocean side of Hilton Head Island.

I couldn't wait to uncork a bottle of wine and dig my toes into the sand.

A weekend alone was exactly what I needed to get my head back in the game.

CHAPTER THREE: Allie

I crossed the William Hilton Parkway, the bridge that connects Hilton Head Island to the South Carolina mainland, just as the sun was setting in the west behind me.

I followed the highway across the island to the Atlantic side. Daddy's beach house was within walking distance of the Port Royal Barony Golf Course. If there was one thing daddy loved more than football, probably more than me, it was golf. That's why he bought this place; so he could literally walk out the door and be at the clubhouse of one of the most beautiful golf courses on the planet without breaking a sweat.

The house itself was rather modest by daddy's means. He was worth a few hundred million dollars and lived in a 27,000 square foot mansion in Bucks County, just outside of Atlanta.

The beach house was around 2,700 square feet. It was a hundred-year-old cottage daddy had restored and tripled in size by adding a second floor and full basement.

There were four bedrooms, three baths, a small gourmet kitchen and living room combination, a walk-in wine cooler, and a deck along the back that was separated from the shoreline by thirty yards of pristine white sand.

Since daddy owned a football team and often lent out the house to his executives and players, he had a construction company dig out a full basement beneath the house to install a large home theater and workout room that had every piece of equipment you could imagine. I wasn't a gym rat (why would you want to lift heavy things?), but I was a runner and sometimes used the treadmill and elliptical when it was too wet or cold to run along the beach.

I blew out a long, happy sigh as I pulled into the driveway at dusk. I put the Audi in Park and leaned in to glance through the windshield. There were lights on in the house, but no cars in the driveway. The three garage doors were closed. I knew daddy kept a Jeep Wrangler in one of the garage bays to drive around the island in the summer, and a couple of Skidoos in another. There was usually one bay empty and that's where I'd normally park.

I opened the console to retrieve the garage door opener, but it wasn't there. I frowned in thought. Shit, I must have given it back to daddy after my last visit. Oh well, I had my key, so I would just go in through the front door and open the garage from inside. No biggie.

I stepped out of the car and gazed up at the dark, clear sky as I stretched the kinks out of my back. The air was thick and moist, but a cool breeze blew in from the ocean to welcome me to the island.

I gazed out at the dark, calm waters and the horizon beyond. The only sound was that of the gentle waves coming to shore.

The horizon was awash with purple light turning to black.

I could see for miles and miles.

There were no storms on the horizon.

Smooth sailing ahead.

* * *

I pulled my overnight bag from the trunk and carried it to the door. When I stepped onto the porch, the motion light above the door came on. I dropped the bag on the porch, then used my key to open the lock. There was a security system keypad mounted on the wall just inside the door. I turned quickly to disarm it, only to find that the alarm was already off.

"What the..." I remembered seeing lights on when I drove up. Maybe someone was in the house. Maybe someone who was supposed to be there. Maybe not. Little tingles of alarm crept up my spine.

My purse was hanging by the strap over my shoulder. I slid my hand inside and brought out the lightweight, Smith & Wesson .38 revolver that I carried with me everywhere I went.

You can preach gun violence to me all day long.

If someone attacks you, feel free to try and talk them down.

Me?

I'm going to shoot the son of a bitch and ask questions later.

I stood in the open doorway and called out. "Hello? Is anyone here?" I turned my year to listen. The house was quiet.

Of course, the house was quiet, you idiot.

Do you think the bad guy is just gonna pop his head out and say, "Here I am!"

I called out again, but got no response.

Maybe the last person to visit left the lights on...

Or maybe they were left on for a purpose, for security maybe...

With my fingers wound tightly around the pistol grip, I took a deep breath and walked slowly through the house, checking the rooms like I saw the cops do it on TV.

I probably looked pretty silly, but better safe than sorry.

I checked the downstairs first, creeping through the living room and kitchen, the downstairs bedroom and bath, the laundry room. The garage door was off the laundry room. I opened the door and turned on the light. As expected, daddy's Jeep was in the farthest bay, and the two Skidoos on a trailer sat in the center bay.

There was a black Land Rover sitting in the closest bay. I stepped down into the garage to take a closer look at it.

I set my hand on the hood. It was warm, meaning the Rover's engine hadn't been off for long. Someone had just parked it here.

I walked around it. The Rover had Georgia license plates and a large Atlanta Trojans sticker on the back window.

The windows were tinted too dark to see inside.

It had big tires and fancy chrome wheels.

I breathed a little easier. I was fairly sure that the vehicle belonged to someone associated with daddy's football team; most likely a player, since all of the execs drove company-issued Mercedes sedans.

The question was, why was the Rover here?

And who the heck was I going to find in the house?

* * *

I continued my search upstairs, checking the remaining bedrooms and bathrooms and finding them empty.

The house had two master bedrooms with attached bathrooms: one downstairs and one up.

In the master bedroom upstairs, there was an Atlanta Trojans travel bag on the bed. The bag was open, so I tiptoed over and peered inside.

There were a couple of t-shirts, a pair of swim trunks, a pair of jeans, a few pair of boxers and socks. A black leather shaving kit was on the bed next to the travel bag. I unzipped it and looked inside.

There was the usual manly stuff: a razor, shaving cream, deodorant, a travel size generic shampoo, and a small bottle of Aramis cologne. I loved the scent of Aramis. One of my marketing professors at college practically bathed in the stuff.

His scent was what first attracted me to him. We ended up screwing like jackrabbits for an entire semester, until he gave me a C in his class.

He told me I was a great fuck, but not a very good student.

Fine. No problem. I understand. Let's fuck.

I took cellphone pictures of him tied naked to a bed with a ball-gag in his mouth and posted them to his personal Facebook account.

Give that a C, motherfucker...

I stole his bottle of Aramis on the way out and never saw him again. I still have the Aramis. It's in my nightstand drawer. I take it out and give it a sniff once in a while when I'm lying in bed getting frisky with myself.

I couldn't resist taking the bottle of Aramis from the shaving kit and holding it to my nose.

A deep voice coming from the door behind me made me jump.

"Find something you like in there?"

I turned quickly with the cologne in one hand and the pistol in the other. The man standing in the doorway with his hands up took my breath away.

He was fortyish, with the lean, muscled build of an athlete, and sandy blond hair that was pushed back from his forehead and plastered with sweat. He was wearing a pair of gym shorts and tennis shoes. His muscled torso was dark from the sun and glistening with sweat. It dripped from his nipples. His shoulders and arms were covered in dark tribal tattoos. He looked like someone I'd meet in my dreams.

He had a towel looped around his neck, holding the ends with his hands in the air. He nodded at the gun I was pointing at him and frowned.

"You don't have to shoot me," he said seriously. "Just take the cologne and be on your way."

I realized I was holding the pistol on him. I looked down at the pistol as if I'd never seen it before. I jerked it behind my back and muttered at him.

"What? No... I..."

He smiled.

My eyes went up and down him.

He had thick muscles in his legs.

The tight gym shorts bulged in the front.

I felt tingly all over.

I forced myself to stare into his eyes.

He worked the towel back and forth across his neck and smiled again. He used his smile like a weapon. It had far more power than the little pistol hiding behind my back.

"I'm sorry. I'm Allie Winston," I said, forcing a nervous smile.

"As in Ben Winston? Owner of the Trojans?"

"Yes, I'm his daughter," I said.

"Awesome!"

He rubbed his right hand on the towel, then stuck it out and smiled again.

"I'm Sam Carson. I'm your dad's new head coach."

CHAPTER FOUR: Sam

I was in the basement gym in Ben Winston's beach house with my earbuds tucked in and Metallica's greatest hits hammering into my brain.

I couldn't hear anything except the heavy metal thunder and the sound of my own breathing as I finished the five-mile run on the treadmill.

I was sweating like a pig. Big drops of sweat ran down my forehead and dripped from my nose. I had a thick towel around my neck. I had to keep mopping my face with it to keep the sweat from burning my eyes.

When the treadmill hit the five-mile mark, it automatically slowed my pace from a full out run to a steady trot. I hit the manual control to reduce the trot to a walk. I clenched onto the treadmill's side handles to steady myself.

My mind chided me to push through another five miles, but my heart and lungs told me I'd had enough.

"You're not a young man anymore, Sam," my agent told me a few weeks back, when the offer to coach the Trojans came through. "Look, you've worked your ass off to get to this point. You've paid your dues for seven years as a quarterback's coach. You've coached two Super Bowl quarterbacks in four years. You've earned your stripes. This is your chance to run your own show. Take this job, stand on the sidelines and boss people around for a couple of years, bank a few million bucks, then fucking retire to the islands."

"Fuck you very much," I wanted to say.

I didn't say it out loud because he was my friend as well as my agent. He was also telling me what I needed to hear, rather than what I wanted to hear.

And he was right.

My body had been beat to hell.

I was pushing myself too hard coaching young quarterbacks, trying to prove that I was still as good as them, even if I could no longer play.

It was time to let others do the hard work while I just called the plays and banked the bucks.

I turned off the treadmill and tugged the earbuds free, then used the towel to wipe the sweat from my face. I glanced at the treadmill's digital readout of my run. Five miles in thirty-five minutes. That's a seven-minute mile.

Not too bad, for someone my age.

I glanced around the room at the various machines that targeted certain muscle groups; the flat and incline benches, the heavy bars and assorted free weights, and the rack of dumbbells that ran the full length of one mirrored wall.

In my playing days, I practically lived in the gym. I would have hit every machine and lifted every weight in the room before stopping.

Now, I was happy to finish the run.

It was enough for one day.

I was feeling my age as I blew out a long breath and headed for the stairs.

I needed a shower, a beer (or six), and whatever I could forage from the freezer. Ben's secretary told me they kept the place fully stocked when she gave me the keys, so I didn't bother to bring any food. She also let her fingers linger on mine for a moment when she handed me the key.

She smiled at me with her eyes and asked if I was going to the beach alone. I said that I was. She said that was too bad.

Note to self: tap that ass when you get home.

I picked up my iPhone and earbuds and turned off the light.

I didn't realize I wasn't alone until I emerged from the basement and heard the floor creaking above my head.

I crept up the stairs as quietly as I could. When I topped the stairs, I saw the backside of a woman in the master bedroom. She was standing at the bed, going through my stuff.

She was wearing a pair of black yoga pants and a loose crop-top over a black sports bra. Naturally, the first thing that registered in my mind was how awesome her ass looked in the yoga pants.

It was the perfect size and shape.

Bubbly, I think the kids call it.

Or a bubble butt, something like that.

I didn't give a shit what it was called. I just wondered what it would feel like cupped in my hands.

Her hair was long and blond. She had it pulled back into a loose ponytail at the back of her neck.

She must be cheerleader, I thought.

Or a player's girlfriend, mistress, or wife.

Or a groupie who followed me here to tie me up and fuck my brains out.

Nah, no way I was that lucky.

If the front of her matched the back, I was going to be a very happy man, either way.

I leaned in the open doorway and flexed my muscles.

I cleared my throat and said something snarky to get her attention.

She gave a little scream and whirled around.

Awesome.

The front did indeed match the back.

She was a natural beauty, with perfect skin and plump lips and blue eyes and little freckles dotting her nose.

It took a moment to realize that I'd scared the shit out of her.

It took less of a moment to see that she was holding a gun and that her hand was shaking.

I held up my hands and gave her a smile.

She tucked the gun behind her back and glanced at my crotch.

Please be a groupie... please... please... please...
Then she told me she was Ben Winston's daughter.
Shit.
Maybe I wasn't going to get lucky after all.

CHAPTER FIVE: Allie

I blinked at him for a moment because I thought I was being punked. I was having a hard time believing that this was Sam Carson, the new Trojans head coach daddy was so excited about.

When daddy told me he was hiring Sam Carson, I assumed that he was talking about Samuel Carson, the sixty-something-year old offensive coordinator for the Chicago Blaze, not Sam Carson, the former college star and professional quarterback known as much for his viral booze and sex videos as for setting passing records in college.

"You're the Sam Carson that's the new head coach of the Trojans?"

"One and the same." He closed one eye and wiggled a finger at me. "Let me guess. You were expecting older, fatter, bushy white eyebrows, big plug of tobacco in my cheek?"

"You know Samuel Carson?" I said, feeling my cheeks flush.

"I should," he said with a nod. "He's my dad."

"Well, that makes sense," I said, even though it didn't. I was just trying to think of something to say to get his attention off the face that he had caught me going through his stuff. "I didn't know that you had left Los Angeles. You were coaching their quarterbacks, I believe."

"You seem to know a lot about football," he said, stepping into the room. He held out his palm and gave me a little nod. I realized that I was still holding the small bottle of Aramis. I set it in his hand and stepped aside so he could get to the bed.

He dropped the cologne inside the shaving kit and zipped it up. I suddenly realized how much I had invaded his privacy. I moved to stand at the door, switching places with him.

"My dad has owned the team for twenty years," I said. "I've been around football my entire life. And it's part of my work."

"Yeah? What do you do for work?" he asked, turning to sit on the edge of the bed.

He stretched out his long legs and pointed his toes. The muscles of his thighs looked like slabs of meat. His calves bulged from beneath his legs. I knew he hadn't played in nearly a decade, but holy shit, he'd held up exceptionally well.

He tugged the towel from around his neck and mopped his neck and chest with it. I watched is swirl over the muscles, across his hard nipples.

I tried to focus. "I work in sports marketing... Image consulting... Public relations... I work with a lot of daddy's players."

"Do a lot of daddy's players need image consulting?" he asked with a playful frown.

I shrugged. "Some do, yes."

"And what about the coaches? Do any of them need image consulting?"

I couldn't resist giving him a smile. "No. You'll be the first."

He made a goofy face and poked his thumbs to his chest.

"You think my image needs work? Seriously?"

I mocked his goofy face and pushed my eyebrows up.

"Well, let's just say that I am aware of your history. In fact, you were used as a case study in one of my marketing classes at Alabama."

"Really? I'm not sure if I should be flattered or horrified." He narrowed his eyes and tapped a finger to his chin. "Let me guess, the case study was called 'how to get drunk and fuck up your career in one night'?"

He was smiling, but I wasn't. The case study I was referring to was how he managed to maintain such a positive image with the fans while seemingly doing everything he could to destroy his career, like the public intoxication, sex romp videos, and innumerable bar fights with fans of opposing teams. I was pretty sure he was talking about the night he got shitfaced and plowed his Lamborghini into the back of an eighteen-wheeler, destroying his shoulder, and ending his career.

I suddenly felt very uncomfortable. I put up my hands and took a step backward toward the door. I had forgotten that the pistol was still in my right hand.

I said, "I'm really sorry I looked in your bag. I didn't know who was here. I saw the bag and..."

"You can make it up to me," he said, flexing his eyebrows. He gave me a devious smile that brought a lump to my throat.

"Uh, how?"

He nodded at the bathroom door. For a moment, I thought he was going to suggest something totally out of the question; at least at this point of our relationship.

"I'm starving, but I need a quick shower because I smell like an old gym sock. Maybe you can shove a frozen pizza in the oven and we can chat over dinner?" He frowned at me. "I mean, if you like frozen pizza."

I smiled. "I love frozen pizza."

"Awesome," he said, pushing himself off the bed. He picked up the shaving kit and took it with him to the bathroom door. He turned back and smiled again. "Should I dab a little Aramis behind my ears?"

He didn't wait for an answer. He gave me a wink and went into the bathroom and shut the door.

I didn't move until I heard the shower turn on.

I fell against the doorframe and let go of the breath I'd been holding.

I brought my hands to my breasts.

My nipples were hard beneath my sports bra.

The crotch of my yoga pants felt like it was on fire.

Sam Carson was the hottest man I'd seen in a long time.

He was also trouble.

His exploits were the stuff of legend in my business.

I hoped my dad hadn't made a mistake in hiring him.

He could be a lot to handle.

In more ways than one.

CHAPTER SIX: Sam

I turned on the shower and let the water run until the bathroom filled with steam. I pried off the tennis shoes and pushed the sweaty gym shorts and underwear down my legs and kicked them aside.

I rubbed the steam off the mirror with the back of my hand, then braced my palms on the sink and leaned in to give myself a good once-over in the mirror.

My body looked good for my age, which was how I had come to measure things now.

You look good, for your age.

You're in great shape, for your age.

You're really attractive, FOR YOUR AGE...

I did look good, dammit, *despite* my age.

I was all lean muscle, toned, with low body fat. My hair had always been a sandy blond, so you had to look closely to see that there were strands of white mixed with the blond.

My face and body were always tanned because when I wasn't on the field, I was on a beach or a fishing boat somewhere.

Little lines cut from the edges of my eyes and the corners of my mouth. I guess I looked okay for a guy on the north side of forty. The ladies never complained, so why should I worry.

As always, my eyes were drawn to the scar that inched its way down the front of my right shoulder. The surgeons had been precise in the cut required to get inside my body and rebuild my shoulder. The tattoos did a good job of disguising it, but I would always know it was there. It represented far more than just a scar. It represented how quickly life could spiral out of control.

I stepped into the shower and lowered my head so the jets could beat against my neck and shoulders.

I felt the tension of the day draining from my body.

I gave my hair a quick shampoo and used the lather to soap up my body. That's how guys can shower so quickly. We use the shampoo to wash everything, unlike women, who seem to have a special soap for every part of the body.

This soap is for my face.

This soap is for my underarms.

This soap is for my cooch.

I was glad that I was a dude.

I washed my cock and balls with the same lather I used to wash my hair. I just saved the dirtiest parts for last.

Speaking of, when my hands swirled the soap around my cock and balls, I wasn't surprised to find my cock plumped up from meeting Allie Winston.

She was a gorgeous girl from all sides.

Not only did she have the bubbly ass, she had nice tits that filled out her sports bra perfectly. I could just see the faint bumps of her nipples beneath the confines of the material.

I had a hard time keeping my eyes off the camel toe wedged between her legs. The yoga pants had worked their way inside her cunt, giving me a nice idea of what she might look like without them.

As the steam swirled around me, I closed my eyes and wrapped my fingers around my cock. I worked my soapy hand back and forth a few times and it quickly grew to its full nine inches. I glanced down at myself. I squeezed as I slid my hand toward the head. The head mushroomed and turned dark.

"Fuck..." I sighed. I braced my left hand on the shower wall and closed my eyes. I could see Allie standing in the doorway, but her clothes were gone. She was cupping her tits in her hands and squeezing her nipples between her fingers. She parted her lips and moaned at me.

I imagined that her cunt was covered in little blond curls.

I could see her swollen clit peeking from beneath the curls.

She put a finger fully into her mouth to wet it, then smiled as she slid the finger between the folds of her pussy. She spread her legs so I could see the finger disappear inside her.

"Yes..." I growled, pumping my cock faster as every muscle in my body tensed.

Her finger slid in and out, in and out.

My hand milked my cock, faster and faster.

I felt myself cumming as the pressure built in my balls, screaming for release.

I stood on my tiptoes and tightened the muscles in my legs.

I bit my lip so I didn't scream.

I shot milky ropes of white cum on the shower wall.

I milked my cock until there was nothing left to give.

I opened my eyes to look at the mess I'd made.

I smiled.

Not bad.

For a man my age.

CHAPTER SEVEN: Allie

I hurried down to the kitchen and hit "Preheat 450" on the oven, then checked the freezer for frozen pizzas. Bingo! The freezer was stocked with every kind of frozen pizza imaginable.

I picked a large meat lovers supreme. I ripped open the box, put it on a pizza pan, and stuck it in the oven. I checked the instructions and set the timer.

I had thirty-five minutes to make myself presentable.

It wasn't that I felt the need to dress for dinner or that I was trying to impress Sam Carson.

To the contrary, the problem was that my panties and yoga pants were glued to my crotch and I could smell the tangy aroma of my own juices wafting in the air.

And if I could smell it, I knew he could.

Men have noses like bloodhounds when it comes to pussy.

They can smell a damp one from a mile away.

I grabbed my bag from the foyer and ran into the downstairs bedroom and slammed the door. I threw the bag on the bed and went into the bathroom for a quick shower.

I turned on the shower to let the water heat up and stripped off the crop top and sports bra. My armpits were drenched with sweat and my tits were clammy, as if I'd just finished a run.

The soggy yoga pants and panties clung to my crotch when I tugged them off.

My cunt was literally gushing.

The musky smell filled the room and made me wonder why Sam Carson had such an effect on me.

Admittedly, it had been a while since I'd had sex, but juicing like a horny teenager was somewhat out of character for me.

I liked to be wined and dined and wooed before giving up the goodies.

I'd had sexual encounters with men I'd just met before, but they were rare, and usually involved tremendous amounts of alcohol and the desire to get out of an ugly bridesmaid dress.

I turned my ear to listen to the shower still running in the upstairs master bedroom.

Sam was in the shower just above me.

Naked.

Wet.

Soapy.

"Stop it, Allie," I scolded myself. "You don't need this. Not now. Not with him."

I pinned up my hair into a bun, jumped in the shower, and quickly soaped up my smelly parts. My fingers lingered on my clit for just a moment, but I quickly pulled them away and rinsed off. I didn't have time for that now. Maybe later, after I went to bed, alone with my thoughts. For now, the fun stuff would have to wait because I wanted to be dressed and in the kitchen when Sam came downstairs.

God forbid he think that I got clean just for him; even though he was the reason I needed a shower.

* * *

I left my hair pinned up in a messy bun on top of my head. I put on a pair of fresh panties, a pair of loose-fitting lounge pants, and a large Atlanta Trojans t-shirt.

My look could best be described as "baggy".

It wasn't that I was trying to be as unsexy as possible.

It just turned out that way.

This was how I dressed when I hung out alone.

Which was still my plan for the weekend.

After the pizza, I was going to politely suggest that Sam find another place to spend the night.

CHAPTER EIGHT: Sam

I could smell the decadent aroma of frozen pizza as I came down the stairs. My stomach growled, reminding me that I hadn't eaten since breakfast. It was nothing that a frozen pizza and a six pack of Coors wouldn't fix. The unexpected company of a lovely young woman would be the icing on the cake.

Or the pepperoni on the pizza.

Whatever.

Allie was setting out two plates on the kitchen table when I came into the room. We looked at each other and smiled. We were identically dressed in a pair of black lounge pants and a grey Trojans t-shirt.

"Okay, this is getting weird," I said with a grin.

"A little bit," she said with a wry smile. "Are you sure you didn't peak down to see what I was wearing?"

"And have the exact same outfit in my bag so I could dress like you?" I asked as I went to the fridge for a beer. I popped the top and toasted her with the ice cold can. "No, my dear, Miss Winston, this is called a coincidence."

"Well, whatever you call it, you look lovely," she said, grinning as she slid the pizza out of the oven.

"As do you."

"Have a seat. The pizza is ready."

I sat at one end of the small kitchen table and watched her pick up the pizza cutter and quickly split the pie into eight pieces. She put two slices on one plate and four slices on another. She set the plate with four slices in front of me and took the two slices for herself.

"I really appreciate this gourmet meal," I said, picking up a slice and blowing cool air across the bubbly cheese. I nibbled off the end and sucked in a quick breath to keep the skin from melting off my tongue.

"Careful, that's hot," she said. She picked up a fork from the table and proceeded to cut her pizza into bitesize pieces. She stabbed a piece and held it to her mouth. I watched her lips purse to blow cool air over the steaming bite.

I picked up the beer and took a sip. Smacking my lips, I said, "So, Allie Winston, tell me about yourself."

She chewed slowly, then picked up the glass of wine she'd poured herself and took a sip. Dabbing her lips with a napkin, she said, "There's not much to tell, really. I grew up in Atlanta, got my Masters in Sports Marketing from the University of Alabama, came back to Atlanta, and got a job with Image Sports Limited. They are based in New York, but I work out of the Atlanta office. I work mostly with athletes in the southeast. I've been there two years and love it."

"Why didn't you go to work for your dad?" I asked.

"Why didn't you go to work for you dad?" she shot back.

"Because my dad's never been more than an assistant coach for shitty teams. And he isn't Ben Winston."

She stabbed another piece of pizza with the fork and gave me the eye. "You haven't worked for my dad for long, have you?"

I shook my head. "Less than a week, but it's off-season so our contact has been minimal. We'll see more of each other when spring training kicks in next week, I'm sure."

"My dad is a wonderful father and a brilliant business man," she said with respect. "But Ben Winston can also be sexist and condescending to his female employees. And to his daughter. I just felt it would be better for our relationship to not work directly together."

"Football is a good old boy's game," I said with a nod. "Although, there are some female team owners now that give as good as they get."

"I'm sure you'd know more about than I would," she said, chewing through a condescending smile. "Weren't you involved with the woman who owns the Huskies? What's her name, Lucinda..."

"Mills," I said, narrowing my eyes at her. "I wouldn't say that I was involved with her."

"Right, right... You just had sex with her in the middle of the day in the owner's box at Huskies Stadium, and a reporter for *Sports Illustrated* who was there to interview you happened to get photos of the two of you on his cellphone." She brought the wine glass to her lips and stared at me from over the top of it. "Or at least that's the story I heard."

"Actually, he was from *Sports Insider*," I said, forcing a smile.

She gave me a condescending smirk. "Ah, my bad. Sorry."

Wow, what a bitch. So much for a nice, civil dinner. This was why I preferred groupies over "normal" women. Groupies don't judge you for the stupid shit you've done in life. To the contrary, they want to fuck you *because* of the stupid shit you've done.

They want to be part of the stupid shit, not run from it and certainly not chastise you for it.

That wasn't the case with Allie Winston—Miss "I Chew My Food a Hundred Times Before Swallowing".

"Word is, Lucinda Mills is a real ball buster," she said casually. She let her eyebrows arch as she sighed into the wine glass. "Did she bust your balls while you were coaching quarterbacks for her, Coach Carson?"

"My balls are just fine," I said. I picked up my beer and leaned back to stare at her. "But to answer your question, yes, Lucinda could be a real ball buster. But then again, most women are ball busters at one time or another."

She put on an innocent face and brought a hand to her chest. "Really? Are we?"

I asked, "Aren't you a ball buster, Miss Winston?"

"I only bust balls that need busting," she said with a dismissive sigh.

"Do you think my balls need busting?" I sucked pizza out of my teeth and held out my palms. "Obviously, you have something to say, so just say it so we can get on with this lovely dinner."

She set the fork aside and laced her fingers together on the table. She cocked her head at me and leaned in a little. "I'm just wondering if all that stuff is behind you now?"

"All what stuff?"

"Oh you know, stuff like public intoxication, sex tapes with groupies and cheerleaders, bar fights with fans from other teams, DUIs, DNA tests to prove paternity..." She smiled curtly. "The stuff that seems to follow you wherever you go, Coach Carson. The stuff my dad will not put up with and the stuff I can't whitewash."

"Ah, that *stuff*," I said. I took a deep breath and blew it out slowly. "Well, Miss Winston, all I can tell you is that *stuff* is in the past. And most of that happened during my playing days. When I wasn't on the field in those days I was either drunk or stoned on pain killers; or on my way to get drunk or stoned. I did a lot of stuff that I'm not proud of, but that's all behind me now."

"Is it?"

My fingers tightened around the beer can until it popped. She glanced at the can and rolled her eyes. If she had been a guy I would have punched the smug look off her face.

I let go of the can and said, "I promised your father that the only headlines I would generate would be related to taking his team to the Super Bowl next year. I gave him my word and that seemed good enough for him."

"Then, that's good enough for me," she said. She picked up the fork and stabbed another bite. "But fair warning; if you thought Lucinda Mills could bust balls, wait till you see what I can do if you try to drag the Trojans through the gutter with you."

I glared at her for a moment, then blew out a long breath and smiled. "Do you put all of your dad's new employees through this drill?"

"Not all of them," she said with the wine glass at her lips. She didn't smile. Her eyes went around my face. "Just the ones who really need it."

I went back to my pizza and ignored her for a bit. I wanted to tell her to go fuck herself, but then I realized that she was right.

I'd spent the last twenty years stumbling drunk and disorderly through the remnants of a once-promising career and life.

It was time to grow up.

The words of my agent echoed in my head.

"This gig with the Trojans is your last shot at staying in the game, Sam. Try not to fuck it up."

CHAPTER NINE: Allie

I honestly didn't mean to start harping on Sam right out of the gate. I'm really not a bitch, regardless of what he was probably thinking now.

But I am super-protective when it comes to my dad and his football team. Not that he needs my help. Daddy wouldn't have hired Sam Carson if he thought there would be problems. Ben Winston was one of the sharpest business men on the planet. If he hired Sam Carson to be the head coach of the Trojans, he had a good reason for doing so. I just couldn't imagine what that reason might be.

Sam and I ate in silence for a while.

He devoured the four slices I'd put on his plate, and then went back for the remaining two slices without asking if I wanted more.

He crushed the beer can and tossed it in the trash on his way to the fridge for another. My wine glass was empty. The wine bottle was on the counter. He didn't offer to retrieve the bottle or refill my glass.

I flipped through the mental card catalog in my mind, trying to recall everything I knew about Samuel Carson, Junior.

Let's see...

Star quarterback at Lincoln County High School in Lincoln, Nebraska...

Set all kinds of Nebraska state high school football passing records his senior year...

Star quarterback at Nassau College in New York his junior and senior years...

Set all kids of NCAA passing records...

Drafted in the first round by the New York Thunder at age twenty-two...

Backed up Kyle Holder, their franchise quarterback, for three years until he retired...

Became the Thunder's franchise quarterback at age twenty-five, and played at the top of his game for ten years, until the night he got drunk and drove his two-hundred-thousand-dollar Lambo into the back of a semi-truck that had stalled on the highway.

His right arm was broken in three places and his shoulder was crushed.

He spent two months in the hospital and a year in rehab, but his ability to throw touchdowns died on the side of that road.

At age thirty-five, Sam Caron's playing days were over.

For the last seven years, he'd worked as a color commentator for ESPN and as a quarterback's coach for three different teams.

And now he was the head coach of the Atlanta Trojans.

Whatever my dad was thinking didn't make a lick of sense to me.

Sam Carson was qualified to coach the quarterbacks and maybe coordinate offense, but to head coach the team, especially after two lousy seasons?

The Trojans needed someone with vast experience in turning shit into diamonds; not someone with experience creating shit wherever they went.

We needed Nick Saban.

Or Jim Harbaugh.

Or Andy Reid.

We didn't need Sam Carson.

What the hell was my dad thinking?

Then a thought crossed my mind.

Ben Winston was no fool.

He knew exactly what he was doing.

Did he hire Sam Carson for his ability to coach a winning team or his ability to generate headlines?

Only my father knew for sure. It was the first question I would ask the next time I talked to him.

* * *

"Hello? Anyone home?"

I shook my head to clear my thoughts. I looked up to find Sam standing next to the table, wiggling the wine bottle at me.

I blinked at him. "I'm sorry. What?"

"I asked if you wanted more wine," he said. He nodded at the empty glass I was holding in my hand.

"Oh, yes, sure. Thanks."

I held out the glass and he put his hand on mine to steady it as he poured. His hand was rough, like sand paper, but warm, like a friendly hug. He filled my glass and set the bottle on the table between us. He popped the top on another beer and took his seat.

I sipped the wine and stole a quick glance at him. He wasn't looking at me. He had his phone out now, fiddling with it.

"I'm sorry," I said quietly. "I didn't mean to bust your balls."

He didn't look up. He shrugged and said, "My balls are tough. They can take it."

I softened my voice in a sad attempt to justify my bitchy behavior. "It's just that, well, the team doesn't need any more negative press."

"I understand." He kept fiddling with the phone. "No problem."

"After Vern Davis was fired as the head coach at the end of last season, and that idiot Malcolm Jamar was caught on video buying crack from a prostitute, well, as I said, the Trojans have had enough bad press."

"There will be no bad press from me," he said, holding up a hand without looking at me. "Scouts honor. I just want to do my job and build a winning team."

He finally glanced up to catch me staring at him. As my eyes focused on his, I felt the doubt and anger draining from my body, replaced by something far harder to control.

The t-shirt fit him much better than it fit me. It was snug on his muscular frame, like a second skin. The round muscles of his shoulders and chest pushed against the thin fabric. The sleeves hugged his thick biceps. The sinewy muscles in his forearms danced as his thumbs tapped on the phone.

"What's up with all the tattoos?" I asked, hoping a change of subject might prove that I could have a conversation without being a ball busting bitch.

He spread out his arms so I could see the sides of his thick biceps. The tats came from his under his shirt sleeves to his elbows. He pushed up his right sleeve to show me his upper arm, which looked as if it had been chiseled from dark stone.

"They are Hawaiian tribal tattoos," he said proudly, pushing up his other sleeve. Christ, if he looked this good as a forty-two-year-old coach, I wondered what he looked like during his playing days in New York.

"Interesting," I said, leaning in to admire his muscular arms as much as the artwork covering them. I resisted the urge to reach under the table to feel his muscle. I mean, reach across the table to feel his arm.

Jesus, have another glass of wine, Allie...

I asked, "Do they have special meaning? Are you part Hawaiian?"

"No. I'm part fan girl," he said with a grin. "I went into a tattoo shop with a picture of The Rock and said, give me those. A few sessions and a few thousand dollars later, I am a walking homage to the great man himself. I have The Rock's tattoos. Or at least as many as I could stand to get. Those fucking needles hurt like a million bee stings."

I blinked at him, waiting for him to tell me that he was joking. The broad grin on his face told me he was totally serious.

"You got all of those tattoos because you liked The Rock's tattoos?"

He took a sip of beer and let his head bob. "Women get their hair done to look like Jennifer Anniston all the time. It's the same thing."

"No, it's not."

"Sure it is."

"Getting your hair done doesn't involved someone poking needles into your body."

He thought about it for a second, then pushed down his sleeves and smiled. "Okay, so maybe it's not exactly the same. But it's kind of the same."

"Kind of," I said. I smiled as I picked up my wine glass and took another sip. I could see why women were attracted to Sam Carson.

He was not only extremely good looking and fit, but he had a casual air about him that sucked you into his world and made you have a good time. Even when you tried not to.

I felt myself swaying in the chair a little. The wine was starting to go to my head. I was exhausted and a little drunk. And always a little horny. I realized I was one glass of wine and one bad bridesmaid dress from jumping into bed with Sam Carson.

It was time for him to go.

I looked around the table. The plates were empty. The pizza was gone. I took a deep breath and said, "Well, this was lovely, but don't let me hold you up."

His handsome forehead wrinkled. "I'm sorry?"

"It's getting late," I said, glancing at the clock on the kitchen wall. "You must be tired. You'll probably want to find a hotel and get some sleep before heading home. Hilton Head has several really nice hotels. Is that what you were looking for on your phone? A place to spend the night?"

"I was choosing players for my fantasy football team," he said, holding up the phone to show me the screen. He shook his head. "I'm not going anywhere. I'm spending the weekend here."

"What?" I shook my head at him. "You can't stay here!"

"Why not?" He made a show of looking around the room. "This place is huge. There's plenty of room for both of us. You won't bother me a bit."

"I came here to be alone for the weekend," I said, gritting my teeth at him.

"So did I."

"I don't want company," I said.

"Neither do I."

He set the phone on the table, then folded his arms over his chest and pushed his eyebrows up.

I folded my arms over my breasts and glared at him.

"You have to leave," I said.

"I was here first," he said.

My mouth dropped open. "Seriously? You were here first? What are you? Twelve?"

"Forty-two," he said. "But I look good for my age."

"What?" I shook my head to make sure I was hearing right. For a moment, I thought he was just fucking with me. "What does how you look have to do with anything?"

"Obviously, not much," he said, pushing his big shoulders up and down. I licked my lips without meaning to. Shit, he did look good, regardless of his age.

"Look, Sam, it would just be inappropriate for both of us to spend the night here," I said. "It really would be best if you left."

"Well, Miss Winston, as you have reminded me all evening, inappropriate is my middle name. So..."

He pushed himself out of the chair and went to the fridge to get another beer.

If he was getting drunk, he wasn't showing it.

His eyes were clear and his walk was straight.

"Where are you going?" I asked as he headed toward the stairs.

"I'm going to bed," he said without turning around. He gave me a little wave over his shoulder. "Good night, Miss Winston. Rest up. I'm sure you'll want to bust my balls some more tomorrow."

CHAPTER TEN: Allie

I sat dumfounded for a moment, waiting for Sam to come back down the stairs with his bag so he could leave me alone.

I heard the bedroom door close.

Two minutes later, I heard the toilet flush.

Then, I heard... nothing...

He had gone to bed.

He really was in for the night.

"Son of a bitch," I said, the words slurring on my lips.

I picked up the wine glass. It was empty. I picked up the bottle. It was empty as well. No wonder I was feeling light headed. I'd drunk the whole bottle of chardonnay myself.

Fine.

Fuck it.

Let him stay.

I'd deal with him in the morning.

I needed sleep.

I set the security alarm and shut off the lights on my way to the downstairs master bedroom.

I closed the door and peeled off my clothes as I dragged my feet into the bathroom.

I sat down naked on the toilet and rested my cheek against my hand.

I closed my eyes and peed for what seemed like hours.

I fell asleep for a moment, then jarred myself awake.

I wiped myself off and flushed the toilet.

I turned off the light and crawled into bed without worrying about pajamas.

Fuck you, Sam Carson, I thought as I drifted off to sleep.

There's a naked, horny woman sleeping in the room right under yours.

A naked, horny woman with great tits and a tight box who hasn't had sex in a while, I might add.

You should have been nicer to me...

You and your big muscles and nice smile...

And your bulging gym shorts...

Fuck you...

Fuck...

You...

* * *

"More wine?"

I opened my eyes.

I was lying on my back in the sand.

I could see the clear blue sky above.

I could hear the surf breaking into shore.

I glanced down at myself.

I was naked.

My breasts were swollen and oiled in a film of sweat.

My pink nipples blossomed and glistened in the sunlight.

Sam was standing above me with the wine bottle in his hand.

He was naked, all muscles and tattoos and sweat.

His cock was long and stiff, stemming from his dark pubes like a snake ready to strike. His cock was veiny and curved upward near the end. The head was like a large mushroom that bloomed before my eyes.

He asked again, "More wine?"

"Yes," I moaned. "More wine."

He tilted the bottle and showered me with red wine from my breasts to my cunt. The wine was cool and felt good in the summer heat. I spread my legs so it could run between my folds and across my taint.

Sam emptied the bottle, then tossed it away. He stroked his cock as he stared down at me with a devilish look on his face.

"Is this what you want?" he asked.

The sky above him began to roll with dark clouds, as if a summer storm was blowing in from the Atlantic.

"Yes, Sam," I moaned, spreading my thighs for him. "I want your cock."

"Where do you want it?" he asked. His cock grew larger as he slowly worked his hand back and forth. I licked my lips in anticipation of having him in my mouth. But first, I wanted his giant cock inside me, ramming me, splitting me open, and pushing me past the point of no return.

"Fuck me, Sam," I said. I clutched my breasts and squeezed them until they ached. "Put your cock inside me, now..."

He lowered himself on top of me...

I could feel his hot skin melting into mine...

I could feel the sand, gritty between our sweating bodies...

I closed my eyes...

I opened my eyes...

Sam was on his back now, lying in a bed with red satin sheets and big red pillows. His cock was standing tall like a ship's mast. My hands were around it, stroking him up and down, watching him grow even longer and thicker from my touch.

"Fuck me, Allie," he moaned.

I climbed on top of him. My pussy was flowing, sending rivers of hot juice running down the insides of my legs. My breasts heaved as I straddled him and slowly lowered my pussy onto the head of his cock.

I braced my palms on his muscular chest and dug in my nails, making him moan. His cock head slid into me, forcing the breath from my lungs in quick gusts. I could feel my pussy expanding for him.

I lowered myself an inch, then two.

Sam put his hands on my hips and roughly forced me down onto him, impaling me fully with his massive cock. I could feel his heartbeat deep inside me, from my cunt to my temples. My heart began to beat to the rhythm of his.

With his hands on my hips, Sam began to lift me up and down, driving me onto his big cock, going all the way in, pushing against my cervix.

"Sam..." I sighed. I'm going to cum..."

"I'll cum with you," he said quietly. His muscles flexed as he easily lifted me up and drove me back down fully onto him.

I squeezed my eyes shut.

I could feel the orgasm building deep within me.

Every nerve in my body went on end.

Sam's cock pulsated inside me.

My pussy grabbed him like a thousand tiny fingers.

"Now..." he said, arching his back to push deeper inside me. "Now..."

I screamed his name and exploded against him.

My juices flowed from my pussy and washed over him, covering his body and drenching the entire bed.

I could feel his warm jizz filling me up.

I could taste him in my throat.

I licked my lips...

I could taste his salty cum on the back of my tongue...

I leaned down to kiss him...

And jarred myself awake.

I looked down to see two fingers of my right hand buried deep inside my cunt.

My hand was covered in my own juices.

The sheet beneath me was hot and wet.

I let my hand slide free, wiped it off on the sheet, then rolled over and went back to sleep.

I'd had enough of Sam Carson for one night.

CHAPTER ELEVEN: Sam

Allie's bedroom door was still closed when I came down the stairs just after eight to go for my morning run. I tiptoed through the kitchen and quietly let myself out the back door. I wasn't awake enough to face her yet, nor did I feel like arguing this early in the morning.

She had a gorgeous face, a great set of tits, and a round, tight ass you could bounce a quarter off of. But sadly, I didn't think Allie Winston and I were destined to be very good friends.

And certainly not lovers.

I didn't have to like a woman to fuck her. After all, I was a guy. Guys will fuck a hot chick whether she likes them back or not. But girls aren't built that way. They don't do hate-fucking. Too bad. They don't know what they're missing. Some of the best sex I've ever had was with chicks I couldn't stand.

Take that, bitch...

Anyway, I was fine not getting added to Allie Winston's buddy list on Facebook.

I had enough friends.

And I had my groupies, so, yeah...

I'd keep off her radar by being a good boy and she could keep off mine by being a bitch.

* * *

The back of the house faced the ocean. The waters of the Atlantic were calm and inviting, tempting me to take a swim after my run. The sky was a bright, cloudless blue. The sun was already well into the sky above the horizon. It was going to be a beautiful spring day.

There was a wide deck that ran across the back of the house, with a set of eight stairs that descended to the beach. The white sand extended thirty or so yards to the edge of the shoreline.

I stood at the bottom of the stairs and took a minute to stretch the stiffness out of my joints.

I grunted like an old man when I stretched these days.

I might look good for my age, but my joints and various injuries – those obtained on and off the field—reminded me that I wasn't a kid anymore.

My battered shoulder ached like a son of a bitch when the weather got cold. Somedays, my back cracked like bubble wrap and my knees popped when I walked. I could practically predict the weather with the aches and pains that crept through the repaired tendons, muscles and bones in my body.

I was wearing the same running shorts and shoes from the night before. The temperature outside was already in the seventies, so I didn't bother with a shirt. I'd let the warm ocean breeze dry the sweat from my body as I ran along the shoreline.

I clipped my iPhone to the waistband and tucked the earbuds into my ears. I flipped through my iTunes library, then chose *The Beach Boy's Greatest Hits* as my musical accompaniment. A fitting selection if I do say so myself.

I glanced back at the house. No sign of Allie.

I took a few deep breaths, then set out across the sand for a quick run.

I'd face off with Allie Winston when I returned.

CHAPTER TWELVE: Allie

Sam was already gone when I got up. I stuck my head out of the bedroom door and listened for a moment, then tiptoed up the stairs and peeked into the upstairs master bedroom. His bag was on the floor and the bed was a mess, so apparently, he hadn't gone far and would be coming back.

I fixed a pot of coffee and poured myself a mug, then carried it out onto the deck. It was a gorgeous day. Bright blue sky. Calm waters. No clouds. A warm breeze blowing in from the ocean. Perfect for my planned weekend of solitude.

I put a hand above my eyes and glanced up and down the beach. This section of beach was private, meant only for the homeowners and their guests. I could see people scattered about the beach in both directions, but I would have the stretch of beach behind the house all to myself.

I had the day all planned.

I would have my coffee, then put on my new red bikini and floppy straw hat, grease myself up like a party pig, then take my book down to the shore to sit with my toes in the sand. Perfect!

And with any luck, Sam would come back from wherever he was and clear out his things before lunch time. Surely he'd figured out by now that he had no business being here alone with me. I mean, I didn't even know the guy. Although I certainly knew of his reputation when it came to women...

Women, hah...

More like groupies...

I settled into a deck chair and took a sip of coffee. Then I remembered the dream. Sam and his monster cock... me with wine all over my naked body... me riding him like a polo pony... my own fingers buried inside me...

My cellphone was resting on the arm of the deck chair. It buzzed and fell onto my thigh, jarring me back to reality.

I picked it up and looked at the screen.

It was my dad on Facetime.

I slid the button to answer the call and held the phone up so he could see my face. I worked up a smile and said, "Hi, dad, how are you?"

He always held the iPhone too close to his face. All I could see was his nose and mouth. I told him to hold the phone away from his face so I could see him better.

"Is that better?" he asked, giving me a goofy grin.

"Perfect."

"So, how's my little girl?" He brought the phone back to his lips to speak, then pulled it away to listen, like he was talking into a walkie-talkie. I rolled my eyes.

"Your little girl is twenty-four and fine." I could hear noise behind him, like an airport lounge. "Where are you?"

He glanced around, then brought the phone to his lips. "I'm still at the owner's meeting in Los Angeles, but I just wanted to give you a head's up about something. Do you know who Sam Carson is?"

I bit my tongue. Boy, did I ever.

At least in my dreams.

"As in Sam Carson, the new head coach of the Trojans?"

"Right. Have you met him yet?"

"No, I haven't. Why?"

"I need you work with him," dad said seriously. "I assume you're aware of his past indiscretions."

"I am vaguely aware," I said slowly. "In fact, I was wondering why you hired him, given his past."

"Ah, those kinds of things don't bother me," dad huffed. "All I care about is rebuilding this damn team. If we have another year like the last two years, well, it could be disastrous."

"And you think Sam Carson is the right choice to help you rebuild the team?" I asked. "Honestly, dad, he wouldn't have been my first choice."

He chuckled and bobbed his head. "You're a smart girl. Don't worry. Sam Carson is just a pawn. He'll be gone before the season starts."

I frowned at the phone, then remembered he could see my face. I put on a blank expression. "I'm sorry. What does that mean?"

"I've been negotiating with Dan Bradford for months," dad said, referring to one of the top head coaches in the business who was reportedly tired of coaching in freezing Minnesota. "He keeps jerking me around, so I threatened to hire someone else and he didn't believe I would, so I called his bluff."

"So you hired Sam Carson to force Dan Bradford's hand?" I shook my head. "Daddy, that's brilliant, but very shitty."

"How is it shitty?" He scoffed at the screen. "Sam Carson will earn a million dollars in severance when I cancel his contract. God knows, that ten times more than he's worth."

"Does Sam know this?" I asked. "That you're just using him to get Dan Bradford to sign?"

"Hell no, and he doesn't need to," daddy said.

"So, what do you need me to do?" I asked the question while dreading the answer. I didn't care for Sam Carson, but I didn't care for my dad's tactics either. It was classic Ben Winston. He used people for his own purposes, then wrote them a fat check to justify his actions and sent them on their merry way.

"I just need you to work your PR magic to make Sam's hiring seem like a much smarter move than it is," he said with a heavy sigh. "I'm getting a ton of crap from the other team owners for hiring him. They think I've lost my mind, hiring a washed-up quarterback coach to head a major AFL team."

"But you haven't lost your mind at all, have you, daddy?" I asked with a sigh.

"No, my dear, I have not lost my mind. Hold on…" The screen went dark for a moment. I could hear him speaking to someone else, then his mouth appeared on the screen again.

"So listen, next week I need you to come to the stadium and meet Sam Carson. Bring a photographer and a good writer. Put together a piece to send to *Sports Insider* or *Sports Illustrated*. Something they can post on their blog right away."

"Seriously, daddy? You want me to put together a puff piece on Sam Carson to justify you hiring him?"

"Of course," he snorted. "He's a good-looking guy. He'll photograph well, and even with all the other bullshit, he has an impressive record as a quarterback's coach. I just need you to justify the hiring so I can tweak Dan Bradford into signing with the Trojans. If Dan is fine with Sam Carson staying on as a quarterback's coach, we'll offer him a job. If not, I'll cut him a check and he can be on his way."

Something down the shore caught my eye.

It was Sam, jogging toward me.

I said, "You really think Dan Bradford is going to fall for this?"

Daddy chuckled and held the phone to his ear. I knew this because all I could see on the screen was his ear and lots of little hairs. The man was a multimillionaire, but would never understand how to use a video phone.

He said, "Honey, for the amount of money I'm offering Dan Bradford, only a fool would pass this up. You just get with Sam Carson and make him look better than he is. I just need him in place until the season starts. Can you do that for me?"

"Of course, daddy," I said, watching Sam get closer. His muscular torso glistened with sweat in the morning sun. I forced myself to look away. "I'll get it done. Whatever you need."

"That's my girl," he said with a grin. "Okay, I have to run. Let me know the minute the story is online so I can call Dan and get things moving ahead."

"Yes, sir," I said. "I love you, daddy."

"Love you, too, little girl."

The screen went dark.

And so did my good mood.

CHAPTER THIRTEEN: Allie

Sam slowed his pace when he saw me sitting on the deck high above the beach. He paused at the bottom of the stairs for a moment to catch his breath. He put his hands on his hips and walked in slow circles with his head down, giving his heart time to slow down and his lungs time to catch up.

I watched him from behind my coffee cup.

He came up the steps from the beach slowly, as if he were approaching a pit viper ready to strike.

He was wearing the short running shorts again.

And no shirt.

His muscled torso looked like he'd been dipped in oil. Sweat coated his chest and shoulders. I briefly wondered what his sweat would taste like on the tip of my tongue. I watched a stream of sweat sluice its way down the center line of his abs and pool at the waistband of the shorts. There was the bulge again...

Earth to Allie... STOP THAT!!

"Morning," he said politely when he reached the top step. He tugged the earbuds from his ears and looped them around his neck. "Sleep well?"

"Very well," I said with a smile. "You?"

"Like a rock."

My eyes went around his handsome face and I suddenly felt a little like Judas. My dad was using Sam Carson like a pawn on a chessboard and there wasn't a damn thing I could do about it. Heck, I had even agreed to help daddy push Sam around the board. I wasn't trying to prevent anything from happening. I was now part of the game.

Sam would be well compensated for his time, but that didn't make what daddy was doing right.

I could tell from the brief time I'd known him that Sam was serious about the coaching job. He wasn't there just for a paycheck like many guys in his shoes might have been. He was there to salvage what was left of his career. And possibly his life. And to help rebuild the team after two disastrous seasons.

I couldn't stop my dad's plan, nor could I warn Sam.

My dad had put me squarely in the middle.

It made me feel like shit.

"There's coffee inside," I said, holding up my cup. I forced my eyes to stay above his neck. "And all kinds of breakfast food."

He wiped the sweat from his face on the back of a muscled forearm and narrowed his eyes at me. "You're okay with me staying for coffee and breakfast?"

I took a deep breath and blew it out slowly. "Look, about last night, you were right. It's a big house. There's plenty of room for both of us. I'm sorry I acted like such a bitch."

A wary smile crossed his lips. "You mean it?"

"I do," I said, holding up my cup. "Get yourself a cup of coffee and come enjoy the sunshine."

He gave me a look of relief, then rubbed his hands together and went inside.

I sipped the coffee and watched a flock of gannets circling in the sky high above the ocean. Gannets were called "missile birds" because they could dive into the ocean at 60 miles per hour to catch fish.

They were circling slowly, looking for fish to swoop down and eat.

The fish had no idea they were in danger.

The innocent looking gannets were the predators.

The unsuspecting fish were easy prey.

Sam Carson was a fish.

So what did that make me?

CHAPTER FOURTEEN: Sam

I had no idea why Allie had changed her mind about letting me stay the weekend at her dad's beach house, but I was glad she did because I didn't want to leave.

The weather was perfect.

The beach was perfect.

And the four young ladies I'd met during my run were perfect; or as close to perfect as twenty-year-old nymphets could be.

One of them, a petite blond with huge tits and a Kardashian ass – Dierdre, I think was her name—told me her dad (a huge Trojans fan) owned the house, and she and her BFFs were there for the whole weekend.

Her BFFs were even hotter than she was.

There was a tall redhead with small tits, but thick nipples that beckoned me from beneath her wet bikini top.

There was a short brunette in a thong that kept licking her lips as she looked me up and down.

And a voluptuous black girl wearing nothing but a towel, with skin the color of dark honey. I could literally taste her on the tip of my tongue.

I thought I had died and gone to Heaven.

"We're having a party tonight," Dierdre said. "You should come."

"Yes, I should come," I said with a smile. "Most definitely."

I promised to see them later and jogged back toward the beach house. When I spotted Allie sitting up on the deck, I cursed under my breath.

Fuck it.

I couldn't avoid her, but I wasn't going to argue with her.

If she wanted me to go I would go.

I would pack my bag and walk back up the beach and spend the weekend neck-deep in teeny-bopper pussy.

Then Allie apologized for being a bitch and invited me to stay.

Wow.

Totally unexpected.

How could I refuse.

* * *

"Did you have a good run?" Allie asked as I sat down in the deck chair beside her with a cup of coffee in one hand and a strawberry Pop-Tart in the other.

"Is there really such a thing as a good run?" I asked with a smile. I stretched out my legs and crossed my ankles. I nodded at my knees. "At the moment, my knees and ankles are telling me what an asshole I am for making them run in the sand. As soon as the feeling returns, I'm sure the rest of my body will chime in."

"You're in really good shape, though," she said.

"For my age."

She scowled at me. "You said that last night. Is that your new tagline? For my age?"

I chuckled and took a sip of coffee. "Yeah, I need to put it on a t-shirt. You look good, for your age. You're in great shape, for your age."

She gave me a scolding look. "Do people tell you that? Or is that just your ego talking?"

I grinned at her. "It's a little early in the day for psychoanalysis, Dr. Winston."

When she smiled, her lips curled up at the edges. I liked her smile much more than her frown, which was mostly what I'd gotten from her so far.

"Have you always been obsessed with age?" she asked.

I gave her a sideways grin. "Only since I got old."

"Forty-two is not old," she said.

"It is in my business," I said with a sigh.

"Forty-two is young for a coach. Pete Carroll is sixty-five. And Bill Belichick is sixty-four."

"How do you know so much about football?" I asked.

"It's my job," she said, shrugging. "The point is, you're one of the youngest head coaches in the league. So, the 'for my age' thing doesn't exactly apply to your career."

"Ah, but it does apply to my life," I said.

"You're only as old as you feel," she said, holding the cup to her lips.

"I'm pretty sure that whoever came up with that one is now dead from old age."

I wiggled my eyebrows at her and she smiled again.

I liked it when she smiled. It made my balls tingle.

We sat in silence for a moment. She sipped her coffee and watched the gannets swooping down to catch fish a mile off shore. I ate the Pop-Tart and brushed crumbs off my chest.

After a moment, she turned in the chair and said, "Can I ask you a serious question?"

I glanced sideways at her. "More psychoanalysis?"

"No, just curious," she said seriously.

"Fine. Shoot."

"Why did you take the job to head coach the Trojans?"

I wrinkled my nose at her. "Why did I take the job to head coach the Trojans?" It was a good question. And one without an easy answer.

I shrugged. "I needed a job and your dad made the offer."

"You made a ton of money during your playing days," she said, as if she had the exact figure in her pretty head. "I seriously doubt that you needed a job."

"Needing a job is not always about needing money," I said.

"So, it's not about the money."

I turned in the chair to face her. "Why are you asking me this?"

"I don't mean to pry," she said, holding up a hand. "I'm just trying to understand the situation."

"The real question you should ask is, why did your dad hire an old quarterback's coach to head his team."

That seemed to stun her into silence for a moment. I took a sip of coffee and smacked my lips.

"It's almost like a bad Kevin Costner movie," I said. "Why did Ben Winston hire Sam Carson when there were so many other better-qualified candidates? I'm Kevin Costner in this scenario. Your dad would be played by Gene Hackman or Robert Duvall."

"My dad looks more like John Goodman," she said playfully.

"Okay, then John Goodman."

She smiled for a moment, then her forehead wrinkled in thought. "Why do you think he hired you?"

I shrugged because I'd asked myself the same question multiple times and still hadn't come up with a logical answer. Ben Winston blew the question off by going on and on about bringing in fresh blood and new ideas and different directions. It was the usual bullshit team owners gave athletes when they didn't want to give them the truth.

I said, "That's a question you'll have to ask him."

She said, "I never question my father's motives when it comes to business. It just pisses him off."

I gave her a wry smile. "But you'll question mine?"

She gave me a smile meant to put me at ease. It didn't. She said, "I'm not questioning your motives. It's just that, well, since we're going to be roomies for the weekend, and will be seeing a lot of each other in the coming months, I just feel like we should get to know each other better. And not just on a surface level."

I took a sip of coffee and glanced at her sideways. "You're in image consultant mode, aren't you?"

"A little, maybe. It is my job." Her cheeks blushed. Her pretty eyes sparkled. "Speaking of doing my job, I'd like to come down to the stadium next week to do a formal interview with you."

"A formal interview?"

"Yes, I can bring a photographer and a writer. We'll put together a piece to send out to *Sports Illustrated* and *Sports Insider*. Something they can post to their blogs. And of course, we'd post it on the Trojans website and across social media."

I shrugged. "Sure, whatever you like. I'm an open book."

"Oh, I'm well aware of that," she said with a smile. "I'll text you and we'll set up a time."

"Sounds good," I said. I drained the coffee cup and set it aside. I leaned to the edge of the chair and stretched my arms high above my head. I grunted as I stretched.

"Wow, you do sound old," she said, trying hard not to smile.

"This old body could use a swim," I said with a long breath. "You wanna come? The water's a little cool, but not bad."

She glanced at my sweaty torso for a moment, then brought her eyes up to mine. "Sure. I'll go change."

She pushed herself out of the chair and disappeared into the house. I got up and headed down the steps to the beach. I could swim in my running shorts. They needed a good washing.

I strolled across the sand and glanced back at the house before wading into the ocean.

There was something very odd about Allie Winston, something I couldn't quite put my finger on. There seemed to be two sides to her. Nice, bitchy. Hot, cold. Fun, serious.

I wondered if there was a third side yet to be revealed.

When I spotted her coming down the stairs to the beach, her big tits bouncing in a tiny red bikini top, I wondered what I had to do to get to know Allie Winston inside and out.

CHAPTER FIFTEEN: Allie

The sun was going down as I stepped into the shower to wash off the film of sweat and sand that covered my body. I was a little surprised to find myself thinking that the day had turned out to be okay.

That wasn't an entirely accurate description.

It wasn't just an okay day.

It was actually a pretty awesome day.

My plans for a solitary weekend went out the window. I had spent the entire day with Sam Carson and I hated to admit it, but I had enjoyed myself immensely.

Who would have thought such a thing was possible?

After our morning coffee-slash-psychoanalysis session, I changed into the new red bikini I'd brought and quadruple-checked myself in the mirror before going out to meet Sam for a swim.

I put my hair up in a ponytail and admired myself in the bathroom mirror.

I had to admit, I looked damn good.

For my age. LOL.

I put my hands on my hips and turned from side to side. My boobs are natural and full, and squeezing them into the bikini top formed a sexy, plump cleavage that made me smile.

I wondered what Sam would think of it.

The bikini bottoms were tiny; just a red triangle to cover my crotch and barely enough material to cover my ass cheeks. I turned my ass to the mirror and looked over my shoulder. My ass was full and round, with no cellulite (yet), thank God. My legs were long and toned from years of running.

All in all, I was pretty damn hot.

And I was sure that Sam would think so.

I'm not sure why I felt the need to impress him now. Last night I had just wanted him to leave me along. But today, he seemed charming and sincere. He seemed genuinely nice.

And Jesus, Joseph, and Mary did he look good without a shirt!

I adjusted the straps around my hips and scolded myself for even thinking such thoughts.

My dilemma was not how to get Sam Carson into bed.

I could probably just snap my fingers and make that happen.

Given his well-documented past sexploits, I was sure Sam would screw anything with a pussy and a pulse.

My dilemma was how to get Sam to realize his situation without betraying my father.

Surely, he must have asked himself how he got the job.

Or asked my father.

Or maybe he didn't ask.

Maybe he didn't want to know the reason why.

Maybe he just took the job in hopes that it would work out the way he hoped.

For all his machismo and bravado, Sam Carson impressed me as man who wasn't as confident in himself as he once was.

Almost dying in a car crash that virtually ends your career and kills your dreams can do that to a man like Sam.

Maybe this job was Sam's last attempt to hold on to what was left of the dream that started nearly forty years ago, the first time he stepped out to play his first Peewee Football game.

By the time I got back outside, Sam was already playing in the surf. He hadn't bothered to change. He was wearing the running shorts and they were soaking wet, which showed off his bulge quite nicely. I could see the outline of his cock beneath the wet material, the shaft long despite the cold water and the round head bulging out. I felt my cunt getting moist and tried to focus my attention elsewhere; like to his thick chest and hard nipples.

Shit.

"You look amazing," he said, standing in water up to his knees. I could feel the heat from his eyes as he checked me out from head to toe. "How did you know red was my favorite color?"

"Another coincidence," I said. I waded into the water until it was up to my waist, then dove in. The water was cool, refreshing, but it did little to put out the fire that was smoldering between my legs.

Sam dove in behind me and we swam out twenty yards and treaded water like two kids in a neighborhood pool.

"It feels wonderful," I said, puffing. "Race you back to shore?"

He smiled with the water lapping at his chin. "I have to warn you, Miss Winston. I'm a pretty fast swimmer. For my age."

"Come on, grandpa," I said. "One, two, three, go!"

I beat him back to the shore by two seconds.

We hung out at the beach for a while. I set up a couple of folding chairs in the sand while Sam brought down a cooler with six beers and a bottle of wine.

He filled a plastic cup with wine for me, and popped a beer for himself.

We sat on the sand, drinking and talking for hours like old friends, until the beer and wine were gone and our stomachs were growling.

I made a couple of chicken salad sandwiches and we ate on the deck. Sam was still in the running shorts and I was in the bikini, both still wet and squishy. I caught him checking out my tits more than once. When my nipples grew hard in the warm breeze, I didn't attempt to hide them from view.

"I met some folks down the beach this morning," Sam said, pointing several houses down. My eyes followed his finger. I could see several bikini-clad young women sunning themselves on beach towels. One of them, a skinny red head, was on her back, topless.

He took a sip of beer and licked his lips. "They're having a party tonight. We're invited."

I cut my eyes at him. "We? Don't you mean, you?"

He shook his head. "I refuse to attend any party without my BFF," he said. "We might be the oldest people there, but it could be fun."

"First of all, I'm not much older than they are," I said, playfully narrowing my eyes at him. "And secondly, I think the invitation was meant for you, not me. You go. Have fun. I'll stay here and chill."

He gave me the smile that made my hot water works turn on. He said, "You have two more days to chill and do nothing. Come on, there'll be music and food and booze."

"And groupies?"

He licked his lips and stuck his tongue into his cheek. After a moment, he grinned and lowered his voice. "Look at it this way, if you come with me, I won't do anything stupid. Like get drunk and make a sex tape with the rainbow girls down there."

I glanced at the girls spread out on the beach. "Rainbow girls?"

"Yeah, one blond, one red, one auburn, one black..."

"Such a man of diversity," I said.

"True, and that's exactly why you should come," he said. He brought the beer to his lips and arched his eyebrows. "God forbid I drink too much and make another viral sex video..."

I drew in a long breath and let it out slowly. I hated to admit it, but he was making sense. Or perhaps I was just trying to reconcile the fact that I wanted to tag along.

I said, "Fine, I'll go, but the moment you do anything to embarrass the team..."

"I know, I know," he said, holding up a hand. "Mommy will make me leave the party." He gave my knee a little pat and pushed himself out of the chair.

"Where are you going?" I asked.

"Big night ahead," he said, wrinkling his forehead and putting a hand to his back. "Grandpa needs a shower and a nap."

He paused in the kitchen door and wiped his hands over his sweaty shoulders, chest and stomach. He held up his hands and went inside.

For a moment, I thought he was going to ask me to join him in the shower and his bed.

Thankfully, he did not.

Because I just might have done so.

I sat there for a moment more, then went inside to take a shower of my own.

A nice, steamy one.

* * *

I took off the red bikini and stepped into the shower.

I let the hot water rinse off the sweat and sand, then reached for the soap.

I swirled the soap across my nipples and sighed.

I closed my eyes and thought of Sam in the shower above me.

CHAPTER SIXTEEN: Sam

I took my usual quick shower, less than five minutes, and stood naked in front of the mirror, toweling off. My shoulders and chest had a red glow from the day spent in the sun with Allie.

It had turned out to be a good day.

A surprisingly good day.

Allie Winston was not the bitch I thought she was.

To the contrary, she was incredibly pleasant and easy to talk to.

She was smart and witty and snarky.

And holy crap, sexy as hell.

It was all I could do to keep my eyes off her tits.

The cleavage...

Those nipples...

They were screaming to get out of that bikini.

Help us, Sam! Free us!

And the bikini bottoms fit her ass like a thong.

The thin strip of red material disappeared in the crack between her perfect ass cheeks. I wanted to pull it out with my teeth. I wanted to chew my way through the crotch of the bikini bottoms and...

My fantasy paused when I heard the shower come on in the downstairs bathroom directly below me. It was an old house with old pipes. When the water came on anywhere in the house, I could hear it.

I thought of Allie stepping into the shower.

Naked.

Hot.

Sweaty.

I closed my eyes and imagined her soaping up her big tits and ass.

Dipping her soapy fingers between her legs.

My cock twitched. I opened my eyes. My cock was hard in my hand. I'd been stroking it without even realizing it.

My brain looped back around.

Allie was in the shower.

Naked.

Soapy.

My eyes opened as a devilish plan came to mind.

Allie was in the shower.

I was not.

I couldn't resist seeing what I could see.

I wrapped a towel around my waist and tiptoed down the stairs, listening as I approached the bedroom door.

My fingers touched the doorknob, expecting to find it locked. The knob turned in my hand. I pushed the door open just enough to peer inside. Across the room, the bathroom door was open. I could hear the shower running. I could hear Allie. She was moaning. My cock grew inside the towel.

I crept across the bedroom and peered around the door.

Allie was in the shower.

The clear glass door was steamy, but I could make out the outline of her body.

She was leaning against the wall with her head back and her eyes closed, swirling the soap around her tits with her right hand.

Her thighs were spread. Her left hand was buried between her legs. My cock stiffened fully. The towel fell from around my waist.

I reached to pick up the towel so I could back out of the room when I heard her call my name. "Sam?"

I looked up to find Allie staring back at me. She was holding the glass shower door open. I could see her body clearly through the steam that was swirling about the room.

She was beautiful, wet, rosy, so fucking delicious.

Her eyes lowered to my cock, which had grown so hard that it ached to be milked.

She held out a hand and said, "Come, let me help you with that."

CHAPTER SEVENTEEN: Allie

I was leaning back against the shower wall with my eyes closed and my legs spread. The water was cascading over my body, down my neck, across my breasts, sluicing into my short blond pubes. I was massaging my breast with one hand and my clit with the other.

Then I heard a noise, faint, almost discernable, like a soft sigh.

I opened my eyes and glanced through the steamy glass shower door.

Sam was standing there, looking very much like the little boy who had been caught with his hand in the cookie jar.

Except this little boy had a long, thick, veiny cock that looked like it was about to burst. I didn't know what to do or say. Should I scream to scare him away? Should I laugh and go on with my shower like it's no big deal? Or should I invite him into the shower with me?

Considering that mere seconds before I was imagining that very cock between my legs, it was not a difficult decision to make.

I opened the door and held out my hand.

"Come, let me help you with that."

Sam blinked at me for a moment, like a deer caught in headlights. He had a towel in his hand, but he made no effort to cover his manhood. I gave him a dreamy smile and wiggled my fingers. "Hurry, before the hot water runs out."

"Are you sure?" he asked stepping closer.

I licked my lips as I stared at his cock. I lifted my eyes to meet his and sighed. "Yes. I want you... I want that... in here... now."

He dropped the towel and stepped into the shower. He put his hands on my hips and roughly pulled me into him. Our bodies melted together under the steamy spray. His hands went around to cup my ass and his lips trailed up my neck and to my mouth.

I put my hands on his cheeks and pulled his mouth to mine. I sucked in a deep breath as his tongue pushed into my mouth and swirled around lips. Our tongues met and it was like sticking a fork in a light socket. A bolt of electricity rushed through me that made my nipples stand on end and my pussy gush. I could literally feel the hot juices dripping from my folds.

Sam's cock was hard against my stomach. I slid my hands down his chest to his cock. My left hand cupped his tight balls and the fingers of my right hand went around his cock. I pressed my thumb to the underside of the head and slowly rubbed up and down the shaft. Sam moaned into my mouth.

His fingers dug into my ass as my hand pumped his cock up and down. I rubbed the tip against my stomach. I could feel the hot trail of jizz left on my skin from the oozing slit.

"God... you feel amazing," he said, his tongue in my ear. His fingers moved from my ass to my breasts. He kneaded the flesh and rolled my nipples under his thumbs. "I love your tits... and that ass..."

"I love cock," I moaned in his ear. My fingers tightened their grip as the skin rolled up and down the shaft. "So long... so hard... I want your cock inside me..."

"Soon," he sighed. He brushed his lips to mine, then bent his knees to trailed kisses down my neck and across my breasts. He pushed me back against the wall and got to his knees. "I want so lick you," he said. "I've fantasized about my tongue in our pussy all day."

I braced my palms against the shower wall as Sam lifted my left leg and set it bent at the knee, over his right shoulder. His left hand slipped beneath my ass to hold me steady as he leaned in and gave my clit a little kiss.

I moaned at the touch of his lips. He swirled his tongue around my clit for a moment, then slid it down between my folds to my asshole and back. I put my fingers in his hair and closed my eyes. He lifted my leg a little more to get the perfect access to my soaking pussy. His tongue swirled around my folds, then he found the little hole and probed in the tip of his tongue.

"Oh... god... Sam..." I moaned. My fingers slid down to his shoulders. "Lick me... Sam... Lick my pussy... Fuck me with your tongue..."

Sam stiffened his tongue and fucked my hole with it until I couldn't hold back any longer. I came is a great gushing wave, squirting hot juice all over his lips and tongue. It drenched his chin and dripped onto his chest. Sam moaned as I filled his mouth with my hot juice. He pressed his lips to my cunt and lapped it up until I couldn't stand it anymore.

"Oh... holy... shit..." I moaned. I reached for him. "My turn."

Sam pushed himself to his feet and we traded places. I pushed him roughly against the wall and dropped to my knees in front of him. His cock was even longer than in my dream. I took it in both hands and pumped it until the head grew dark crimson. I put my lips around the head and tongued the slit. His salty ooze covered my tongue. Sam shuddered against the wall.

"Yes... Allie..." he moaned. "Yes..."

I opened my lips and took as much of him into my mouth as I could. I leaned into him and only stopped when the tip of his cock hit the back of my throat. I resisted the urge to gag.

I held his cock steady and started sliding my mouth back and forth over the shaft. As I mouthfucked him, my other hand went under his balls and found his asshole. I teased him, sliding in the tip of my finger, then a little more.

"God... I'm going to... explode..." he said. He leaned down and put his hands under my arms and easily lifted me up.

He pulled me to him and kissed me hard.

He pushed me against the wall and lifted my leg up again, exposing my pussy to the head of his throbbing monster cock. I took his cock in my hand and pulled him to me. I guided the head to my opening and gave him a dreamy smile.

"Fuck me, Sam. Fuck me hard."

He kissed me again, and when his tongue slid into my mouth, he buried his cock hard into my pussy. The breath rushed from my lungs when I felt the tip of his cock hit my innermost wall. He rocked his hips, thrusting in and out, forcefully impaling himself into me.

I laced my fingers around the back of his neck and held on for the ride. Sam pounded his cock into me, hard and fast. I panted like a dog, exhaling as each thrust forced the air from my lungs.

Sam closed his eyes and pressed his forehead to mine. I opened my eyes to watch him as the orgasm started to build. His forehead furrowed. The skin around his eyes tightened. He gritted his teeth and sucked in gasps of air between them.

The smoldering fire that was inside my body became an inferno. Sam's cock was stretching my pussy, awakening new nerve endings. I could feel him in my throat, in my breasts, in my soul.

"I'm cumming..." he moaned, his hips piledriving into me.

"Cum, my darling..." I said. "I'm cumming... with you..."

I felt Sam's entire body tense as his muscles tightened and he thrust into me as deeply as he could go. I felt my pussy contract around him, milking him, drawing out the hot, milky seed that was filling me to overflowing.

I came against him, squirting juice over his cock and balls, hot and sticky. I could feel our juices mixing and running down the inside of my legs.

After a moment, we clinched one last time, and released the deep breaths we'd both been holding. Sam lowered my leg and I squeezed my thighs together to keep his cock inside me.

"That was... amazing..." he said, his lips at my ear.

"Yes... it was," I sighed. "Do you still want to go to that party? It would be a shame to disappoint your rainbow girls."

He gazed into my eyes, then rubbed the tip of his nose to mine and smiled. "Actually, Miss Winston, I'd much rather spend the rest of the weekend right here. Alone with you."

I pulled him close and cooed in his ear. "I think that can be arranged. Coach Carson."

CHAPTER EIGHTEEN: Sam

When I first arrived at Ben Winston's beach house, I had no grand plan for the weekend other than to kick back, relax, get drunk, and maybe have a little fun with a local lady or two.

I certainly did not expect to meet an amazing woman who could make me laugh, make me mad, and make my toes curl all in the same breath.

Allie Winston was unlike any woman I had ever met.

She was beautiful, strong, independent, smart, funny... and right at the top of my "Best Sex Ever" list. Yes, men keep track of such things. And hitting Number One was no small feat, given the number of women I'd had sex with.

We spent the rest of the weekend eating, drinking, swimming, sunning, and fucking. We did not leave the house, except to take a moonlight skinny dip in the ocean, which resulted in moonlight sex on the beach.

And we didn't bother putting on clothes until it was time to leave on Monday. There was no need. As fast as we'd put clothes on, we would just rip them off again.

It was an incredibly wonderful, incredibly exhausting weekend. I truly liked Allie. A lot. So much so, that I wanted to spend more time with her when we got back home. There was a spark there that neither of us could deny. I couldn't believe that I, the eternal bachelor and commitment-phobe, was wondering if we might someday be something more than weekend lovers.

I had to head back to Atlanta on Monday afternoon, so I left that the morning. Allie didn't have to be back at work until Tuesday, so she was going to lounge around for a few more hours before heading home.

"I had a lovely weekend," she said as I tossed my bag into the back seat of the Land Rover. I closed the door and took her into my arms.

"So did I," I said with a smile. I kissed the tip of her nose. "Who knew that the bitchy girl who served me frozen pizza would turn out to be so fucking nice?"

She gave me a scolding look. "And who knew that the obnoxious guy with the big bulge in his gym shorts would turn out to be so fucking nice?"

"Guess we're both a little in shock," I said, pulling her close. "Can I see you when you get back in the city?"

"Just try to avoid me," she said. She put her arms around my neck and pulled my lips to hers. She gave me a gentle goodbye kiss and slowly pulled away.

She said "I'll also text you about the interview for *Sports Illustrated.* Maybe we can do that on Tuesday afternoon."

"Works for me," I said. I opened the door and climbed in behind the wheel. I paused to smile at her.

"Bye, Allie Winston."

"Bye, Sam Carson."

She leaned in through the open window and kissed me again, then gave a little wave as I drove away.

CHAPTER NINETEEN: Allie

I forced a smile as I watched Sam drive away. When the Land Rover was out of site, I clenched my fists and shook them at the blue sky.

"Fuck!" I screamed. "Jesus, Allie, what the fuck are you thinking?"

I shook my head as I went back inside the house. I had to be insane, getting involved with the man my dad was using as a pawn; a man that I had developed strong feelings for in a very short time.

I wasn't falling for Sam Carson, but I liked him.

A lot.

He really was a nice guy. He was also charming and funny and sexy and amazing in bed. I'd had my share of lovers, but no one had ever made me feel like Sam made me feel. It made me sad, knowing that our romance would be short-lived. When Sam found out that I was helping my dad, he would probably never speak to me again.

Two days ago, that wouldn't have bothered me in the least.

But now, after two days in his arms, the thought of Sam never speaking to me again was enough to make me cry.

CHAPTER TWENTY: Allie

I sat in the back of the training room fiddling with my phone while the writer interviewed Sam for the blog piece we'd push out across all media later in the day. I had briefed the writer, who was being paid to write exactly what I told him to.

It would be a puff piece about the handsome, former Pro Bowler and quarterback's coach who had gotten the top job as the Trojans' head coach despite fierce competition and little experience. The piece would completely ignore Sam's notoriety as a bad boy womanizer and hard drinker. It was an old PR trick: bury the bad, promote the good, and rely on the short attention span of the American public to believe what you tell them to.

There would be a quote full of clichés from my dad about injecting new blood into the team, taking a fresh approach, and the desire to lead the team in a new direction (since the old one hadn't worked in years).

The photographer took candid shots during the interview, then took a posed shot of Sam standing in front of the Trojans logo on the wall, holding a football between his hands. He looked strong and handsome, confident, like Hector standing at the gates of Troy; ready to defend his kingdom against Achilles and all comers. Sadly, Hector did not live to see victory. I took a deep breath and pushed the analogy from my mind.

"All done, Allie," the writer said as he and the photographer came my way.

"Did you get everything you need?" I asked.

"Yes. I have the quote from your father and the notes you sent over. I'll get this written up immediately and sent to you for approval."

"Great," I said with a sigh. "I'd like to have it go out as soon as possible." I looked past the writer at Sam. He was standing at the front of the room chatting with two of the assistant coaches left over from the old regime. Sam was smiling and laughing like he didn't have a care in the world.

He had no clue that the interview he'd just done would probably be seen as the obituary for his career.

CHAPTER TWENTY-ONE: Sam

"Did you see the piece on the *Sports Insider* website?" Allie asked. Her pretty face loomed large on the big computer monitor on my desk. "They posted it last night and they already have over fifty-thousand hits."

"What are you wearing?" I asked, leaning in and pretending to peep down the front of the screen. I flexed my eyebrows at the webcam. "Come on, show me your tits."

"You're awful," she said with a smile. "I'm at my office and there's a strict no flashing rule. Sorry."

"Come on, you show me yours and I'll show you mine," I said.

"I don't think yours would fit on my screen," she said with a devilish grin.

I smiled; something I'd found myself doing a lot since meeting her. I asked, "Do you wanna grab dinner tonight?"

"Just dinner?" she asked.

"Now who's awful." The office phone on my desk buzzed. The caller ID read: Ben Winston. "Hey, let me call you back. I have a call coming in."

"Okay, sounds good," she said. She gave me a smile, but there was a touch of tension in her voice. "Sam?"

"Yes."

She sighed and shook her head. "Nothing. I'll see you tonight."

"You got it." I turned off the monitor and pressed the button to answer the desk phone. It was Ben Winston's secretary; the one I had thought about screwing when I got back in town. Crap, I was going to have to let her down easy. I was only interested in screwing one woman now. And it wasn't her.

"Sam, Mr. Winston would like to see you right away in his office," she said formally. There was no hint of flirtation in her voice. Maybe I had misread the signals. It certainly wouldn't have been the first time.

I said, "Sure, I'll be right there."

I hung up the phone and whistled happily as I walked to the elevator that would take me up three floors to the executive suites. Ben must have seen the interview and wanted to congratulate me in person. I was the new face of his team. I was sure he just wanted to hear that I was going to do my best not to let him down.

I sighed happily as I stepped into the elevator and pressed the button. Life was pretty damn good.

New job, new girl, new day.

Maybe I wasn't going to fuck things up after all.

* * *

"You can go right in," the secretary said without looking me in the eye. She nodded at the closed door that had Ben Winston's name on it. I didn't bother knocking. I opened the door and breezed in like I didn't have a care in the world.

"Sam, thanks for coming up so quickly," Ben said, coming around the desk with his hand extended. He shook my hand and motioned me to sit in one of the two chairs in front of his desk. There was a skinny man in an expensive suit in the other chair. He stood up and held out his hand.

"Sam, do you know Earl Holly, our in-house legal counsel?"

"No, nice to meet you," I said, shaking his hand.

"Likewise," he said.

We both sat down as Ben went back around the desk and lowered himself into the high-backed leather chair. He laced his fingers together on the desk and gave me a smile.

Allie must have gotten her looks from her mother, because she looked nothing like her father, thank god. He was a big man with a ruddy complexion and salt and pepper hair that he wore slicked back like a mobster. He had deep set, dark eyes that closed when he smiled.

He cleared his throat and said, "So, Sam, the reason we called you up here is to let you know that something has come up and we're going to need to make a change."

"A change?" I glanced sideways at the lawyer for a moment. Any time there was a lawyer in the room I got nervous. "What kind of change?"

Ben took a deep breath and blew it out slowly. "Well, to be blunt, Sam, we've decided to hire Dan Bradford to head coach the team this year."

I blinked at him. "Um, didn't you already hire me for that job?"

"The contract was never finalized," the lawyer said in a nasally voice that sounded almost like a cartoon character.

I frowned at him. "What does that mean exactly?"

"It means that the contract was sent to your agent for you to sign, but was never returned to us, therefore, the contract is invalid."

"I signed the contract," I said.

"Are you sure?" the lawyer asked.

"I..." No, I wasn't sure. I vaguely remembered a voicemail from my agent about getting my signature on something... Shit.

"Anyway, Sam, it's a moot point. The contract was never returned to us, so the contract is invalid."

"So, you're firing me?" I said it calmly, but my insides were churning. My fingers gripped the arms of the chair. I was losing another job before even having the chance to step onto the practice field.

"Technically, you're not being fired because you were never hired," Ben said with a shrug. "We've been after Dan Bradford for a while now and he decided this morning that he'd like to come to Atlanta. He's tired of the weather in Minnesota."

"Dan Bradford is taking my job." I said it quietly to myself.

"Technically, it was never your job," the lawyer echoed.

I shot him a look that made his mouth snap shut. One good elbow would drive his nose into his face and send him reeling. He seemed to read my thoughts. He shut his mouth and looked to Ben for help.

"The good news is that Dan would like to talk to you about coaching his quarterbacks if you're interested in staying on with the team." Ben gave me a placating smile that made my blood boil. "We could discuss salary if Dan decides to bring you on."

I looked him in the eye and nodded slowly. "I appreciate that, but I think I'll pass."

Ben held out his hands. "Well, that's certainly your call."

I was still nodding, thinking. "Funny, the timing of all this."

Ben narrowed his eyes. "How do you mean?"

"I mean you make the offer to me two weeks ago, but you just said you'd been after Dan Bradford for a while."

Ben glanced at the lawyer, then back at me.

He said, "Yes. So?"

"Then the interview about me being the new head coach gets blasted all over the internet, then Dan decides to come to work for you the next day."

Ben shrugged it off. "Coincidence. Timing. Call it what you will. Either way, we're not going to be needing your services."

"I understand." It was clear by the tone of his voice that it was a done deal and there was no point in arguing. The question I had was, who else was in on the deal?

"You used me," I said quietly. I fixed my eyes on his. "You used me to get Dan Bradford to sign with you."

"There is the matter of severance," the lawyer said.

"Ah, yes." Ben reached inside his jacket and brought out an envelope. He slid it across the desk to me. "That's for you."

I picked up the envelope and looked inside. There was a check for one million dollars. The check wasn't signed. I held it up. "What's this for?"

"We'll need you to sign a document that states, once you accept this check, you'll pursue no other legal recourse against the Trojans."

"Legal recourse?" I cut my eyes between them. "If my contract was invalid as you say, I have no legal recourse. So, why are you paying me off?"

"It's not a payoff, Sam," Ben said, holding up a hand to cut the lawyer off. "Let's just say I feel terrible about how things have ended up. That's just my way of showing you my gratitude. Once you sign the document, which is merely to tie up loose ends, I will sign that check and you can be on your way."

"I see." I nodded slowly and tucked the check back into the envelope. I asked the question that had been nagging at the back of my mind. "Did your daughter know what you were doing?"

Ben's forehead furrowed. "Allie?"

"Yes, Allie." I set the envelope on his desk. "She seemed a little distracted when I was talking to her earlier in the day. I sensed something was up. I'm just wondering if she knew what you were up to."

He shrugged. "Allie and I work very closely together."

"If you want me to sign that paper saying that I won't for breach of contract, you'll answer my question," I said. "Did Allie know that you were using me to get Dan Bradford?"

Ben exchanged a glance with the lawyer. He nodded and the lawyer gave me the document to sign. Then he gave me a pen. I set the document on the desk and held the pen to the signature line. I stared at Ben.

I asked again, praying that he wasn't going to confirm my suspicions. "Did she know?"

Ben blew out his cheeks and spread his hands. "As I said, my daughter and I work very closely together. Of course, she knew."

I pushed the check at him. He took it out of the envelope and we signed at the same time.

I slid the signed document across the desk and he handed me the signed check.

And with that, my brief career as the head coach of an AFL team came to an end.

And so did my brief infatuation with Allie Winston.

CHAPTER TWENTY-TWO: Allie

"Allie, turn on ESPN, quick!"

I looked up to find Darcy, my personal assistant, standing in my office door with an alarmed look on her face. I picked up the TV remote from the desk and aimed it at the flat screen mounted to the wall.

"Breaking news out of Atlanta today," the Playboy model turned ESPN anchor said, doing her best to put a serious look on her perfect face. "Sam Carson has been let go as the Trojans head coach after only two weeks on the job. Taking his place, legendary coach Dan Bradford, who will become the highest paid AFL coach at a reported salary of seven-million dollars a year. Trojans owner Ben Winston has scheduled a press conference for three o'clock eastern time today. We will of course carry that press conference live here on ESPN."

I watched the report with my mouth hanging open. I knew it was coming, but I was still dumbfounded.

Darcy gawked at me. "Did you know?"

I gave her a little nod. "Yes."

"Wow, poor Sam Carson," she said. "Do you want me to get your dad on the phone? I'm sure he'll want you at the press conference."

I shook my head. "No, I'll call him." I forced a smile. "Thanks. Please close my door."

I waited until she left to start crying. I didn't need to talk to my father. I needed to talk to Sam. I could only imagine how he must be feeling. Especially if my father told him that I knew about his nefarious plan all along.

* * *

I called Sam's cell, but it went straight to voicemail.

I called his agent, Alan Dunleavy, but his secretary said Alan was in meetings all day and wasn't taking calls. I left a message, but knew that my call would never be returned.

Sam hadn't been in town long enough to find a place to live, so he was staying at the Atlanta Marriott downtown. I called and asked to be connected to his room. The desk clerk told me that he had checked out and hour before.

My cellphone buzzed on the desk. It was my dad, probably calling to see if I was coming to the press conference. I let it go to voicemail. At this point, I didn't know what I was going to do.

I pushed myself away from the desk and went to stand at the wall of windows that looked out over downtown Atlanta. I had tears in my eyes. My view was blurry. Sam Carson was out there somewhere, but I had no idea where. I just knew that no matter where he was, I was probably the last person on earth he wanted to talk to.

CHAPTER TWENTY-THREE: Sam

I was born and raised in Tipton, Nebraska, a nondescript little town on the outskirts of Lincoln. My mom still lived there in the same house I grew up in; a hundred-year-old farmhouse in the middle of three hundred acres of corn. My family didn't grow corn anymore, not since mom's dad died. She leased the land to neighboring farmers who worked it. I think she often regretted not marrying a farmer who would stay home and raise crops. Instead, she married a football man who was never home and raised hell.

I had offered many times to buy her a new house anywhere on the planet, but she always refused. Her roots ran deep in Tipton, she said. She couldn't imagine living anywhere else. She never said anything, but I know she was disappointed that I'd severed those roots so easily and never looked back.

My dad technically still lived there, too, but he was rarely home. He had been a coach for four decades, and that meant he had to go where the job took him. He was home a few months a year. The rest of the time, he was on the road.

I heard him tell a buddy once that the only time he was truly happy was when he was on the football field. I used to hate him for saying that, then I came to understand. Football was in our blood. We had to be in the game in some capacity or we would go mad.

Dad was in Chicago now, working as the offensive coordinator for the Blaze. He was in his sixties. He smoked like a chimney and drank like a fish. He popped Viagra like Tic Tacs and screwed any woman that would have him. And he had no intention of every retiring.

"I'll die on the sidelines," he told me. "I just hope they wait until after the game to haul me away."

* * *

"More coffee, dear?"

My mother refilled my cup without waiting for me to answer. I looked up with a sleepy smile and said thanks. She set the pot on the stove and took the chair across from me. She frowned at my half-eaten breakfast plate.

"You didn't eat much," she said.

"I ate enough," I said with a smile. "You know, mom, I'm not eighteen anymore. I can't eat a dozen eggs all by myself."

"You have to feed the machine," she said with a smile. Her eyes sparkled behind the cat-eye glasses she wore. "Isn't that what you used to say when I'd catch you and your football buddies cleaning out my fridge?"

"Well, the machine can't eat the way it used to," I said with a sigh. I leaned back and rubbed my belly. "And this machine will get fat as a pig if you keep feeding it like that."

She picked up her cup and held it between her hands. She gave me the same concerned look I'd been getting since suddenly showing up on her doorstep three weeks before. "So, what's on your to-do list today?"

I shrugged and scratched my chin, which was covered in a week's worth of stubble. "I don't really have a to-do list," I said. "Is there anything I can help you with here?"

She took a slow sip of coffee and licked her lips. "No, dear, I think you have fixed everything that needed fixing. You can feed the chickens if you like. The feed is in the bin in the barn. And gather the eggs while you're out there."

"I can do that," I said. "Feed the chickens, gather the eggs."

She smiled for a moment, then let the smile fade from her lips. "What's your plan for going back to work?"

I blinked at her. "I don't have a plan," I said with a shrug. "I'm rich, mom, I don't have to work."

"You're also a lot like your father," she said, although I wasn't sure she meant it in a good way. "Football is in your blood, Sammy. You will never be satisfied to just watch it on TV."

She reached a hand across the table to pat my arm. "Don't let what happened in Atlanta keep you from doing what you love, dear. You're still a young man. There are lots of things you can do to keep your hand in the game. I always loved watching you on ESPN. So handsome in your little suit and tie."

"I know, mom," I said, rolling my eyes. My mom will always see me as ten years old. "I just need a little break, that's all."

"Well, I'm sure you'll figure it out," she said. "In the meantime, I'm thrilled to have you home. Stay as long as you like."

"Thanks, mom," I said. She got up and started clearing the dishes. She set the dishes in the sink and turned on the faucet, then glanced out the window as she waited for the water to warm. "Who could that be this early in the morning?"

I finished the coffee and carried the cup to the sink. I followed her gaze out the window. There was a car coming down the mile-long dirt driveway from the main road. The sun was glaring off the windshield, so we couldn't tell who was in the car.

"I don't recognize the car," mom said.

"I'll see who it is," I said, giving her a kiss on the cheek.

I licked the coffee from my lips and went out the front door. I leaned against one of the columns next to the front porch steps and watched the car approach. The car was a black Chevy. It had an Avis Rental Car tag on the front. The driver pulled to the end of the drive and shut off the engine. The door opened and a woman wearing khaki shorts and a blue crop-top stepped out.

It was Allie Winston.

"Hi," she said, walking toward me with a timid smile on her face. "I've been trying to call you, but keep getting a message that the call won't go through."

"There's no cell service here," I said. I crossed my arms over my chest and gave her a blank look. "What are you doing here?"

"I wanted to talk to you," she said. She came to stand at the bottom of the three steps. Her long hair was pulled back and clipped above her ears. Her face was radiant, rosy. Her lower lip quivered, as if she were fighting to hold back tears.

"How did you find me?"

"Your dad told me you were here," she said. "Can we talk?"

"You wasted a trip," I said. "There's nothing to talk about."

"Sam, please, you have to understand..."

"Who is this?" My mom came out the screen door, drying her hands on a dish towel. She looked at Allie and smiled. "Hi, I'm Evelyn. Are you a friend of Sam's?"

"Not really," I said. I nodded at Allie. "This is Ben Winston's daughter, Allie."

Allie tried to smile.

Mom didn't.

"Your father is a horrible man," mom said, wagging her finger at Allie. "To do what he did to my son. Who treats people like that? He should be ashamed of himself."

"That's exactly what I told him, Mrs. Carson," Allie said, her head bobbing in agreement. "My father is a good man, but he can do some pretty despicable things."

"Are you here to apologize for him?" mom asked. She folded her arms over her chest, mimicking me, and stood next to me on the porch, a united front.

"No," Allie said, looking at me with tears in her eyes. "I'm here to apologize for myself."

* * *

Allie asked again if we could talk.

I said no and told her to leave.

My mom sensed that there was something more going on between Allie and me. She glanced at me for a moment. She had been married to a football man for four decades. She knew what hard-headed schmucks we could be.

"Don't be rude, Sam," mom said, bumping me with her elbow. "She seems like a very nice young lady. You should hear her out."

"Yes, Sam, please," Allie said. "Just give me five minutes."

I took a deep breath and blew it out slowly. I went down the steps and nodded toward barn where mom kept two milk cows and a coop full of chickens.

"Fine. Come on. You can talk while I feed the chickens. Then you can go."

CHAPTER TWENTY-FOUR: Allie

My heart literally skipped a beat when I got out of the car and saw Sam standing on the porch. I wasn't sure how I expected him to react.

Would he take me in his arms and forgive me for what I'd done? Or would he turn me away and say that he never wanted to see me again.

I wouldn't blame him if he turned me away.

I wasn't sure I would forgive me, if I were in his shoes.

I followed Sam to the barn and watched as he scooped ground corn from a bin, then leaned over a fence to scatter the feed on the ground. A dozen chickens flew down from their roosts in the rafters and attacked the feed. It reminded me of watching the gannets dive for fish off the coast of Hilton Head. God, that seemed like a lifetime ago...

"Okay," Sam said, dusting the feed off his hands. "You have five minutes. Let's hear it."

I took a deep breath and gave him the speech I had been practicing in the rental car for the past hour. "Sam, I think what my father did was awful. And I'm sorry if I played any part in it."

"If?" He scoffed and shook his head. "That's your apology?"

"Okay, fine. When I found out what he had planned, I should have told you, but you have to understand, I was caught in the middle. He's my father and you... well, I didn't really know you at all. He asked me to set up the interview and that's all I did. Honestly, I hoped the interview would convince him that you were the better choice. I didn't think Dan Bradford would actually sign."

He rolled his eyes at me. "Are you going to waste your five minutes feeding me bullshit, Allie? Or are you going to tell me the truth?"

"I'm telling you the truth," I said desperately.

"When did you find out what he had planned?"

I blinked at him. "When?"

"You just said that he wanted you to set up the interview. You mentioned that to me before we ever slept together."

"I did?"

He widened his eyes and gave me a slow nod. "You knew what he had planned. That's why you slept with me." He put his hands to his head. "Oh my god, you fucked me to keep me pacified till your daddy could get Bradford signed!"

"What? No, that's not the way it happened."

"Daddy told you to keep me happy, so you fucked me all weekend, did the interview, then got out of his way. I'll be a son of a bitch."

My mouth moved, but no words came out. I didn't know what to say. He was right about the way the events played out, but not about my motives to be with him.

"You're wrong," I said, tears welling in my eyes. "I slept with you because I wanted to. It had nothing to do with my father."

"Bullshit," he said, waving his hands at me. "You're as big of a liar as your old man." He turned away from me and shook his head. "Just fucking leave me alone, Allie. I took your dad's payoff and I got to fuck his daughter. Not a bad payday really. So just get in your fucking car and leave. You don't have to pretend to like me anymore."

"I'm not pretending, you fucking idiot!" My voice cracked and filled with tears. "Dammit, Sam, would I come all this way if I didn't..."

He turned to face me. "If you didn't what?"

I took a deep breath and blew it out slowly. I wiped my nose on the back of my hand. "Would I come all this way if I didn't love you?"

He gave me a look of disbelief. "You love me?"

"Yes. I mean, I think so."

He shook his head. "I don't understand, why are you telling me this?"

"I'm telling you because it's true," I said, moving closer to him. "I know it sounds insane, but the weekend I spent with you... the things we did... I can't get you out of my mind, Sam. And yes, I think I love you."

Sam narrowed his eyes and let them go around my face. His eyes settled on my lips.

"You did a really shitty thing," he said.

"I know."

"I'm still mad at you," he said.

"I know."

He gazed into my eyes. "You really love me?"

I smiled. "I really think so."

He held out his hands. "Show me."

I melted into his arms. I stood on my tiptoes to press my lips to his. I inhaled deeply as our tongues danced. I was immediately overcome with his scent. Aramis. I could smell it on his clothes and on his skin.

"Up there," he said, breaking the kiss long enough to lead me to a ladder that rose into the hay loft above us. I scurried up the ladder with Sam close at my heels.

He pushed me onto a bed of soft hay and tugged his t-shirt over his head. He shimmied out of his jeans and underwear. I sighed when I saw his cock, stiff and ready, waiting for me.

"What about your mom?" I asked as he tugged the shirt over my head. I shrugged off the bra, then slid the khaki shorts and panties down my legs and leaned back with my thighs spread.

"She's allergic to hay," Sam said with a smile, lowering himself on top of me. He kissed my lips with abandon as his hands kneaded my tits and his fingers rolled my nipples. I moaned into his mouth and reached for his cock. God, it felt so good in my hands: hard, long, throbbing. I pumped him for a moment, then pulled him toward my wet pussy.

"God, you feel so good," I sighed as the head of his cock slid into me. I reached around to cup his ass in my hands and pulled him fully into me. I gasped and wrapped my legs around him.

"I missed you," he said, panting in my ear. He braced his palms next to me and started moving his hips in and out, in and out. I could feel him filling me completely. My pussy engulfed him, clung to him, milked him for his hot seed.

I brought my hands to my tits and squeezed until it hurt. My nipples were hard as rocks between my fingers. Sam pummeled into me. His cock impaling me fully, driving the breath from my lungs, making my breasts bounce in my hands.

"I'm... cumming... Allie..." he moaned.

I laced my fingers around the back of his neck.

"Fuck me hard... Sam... Make me cum...

Sam took the challenge. His thrusts grew faster and deeper. I could feel the orgasm tearing through my body, ripping across my breasts and shooting out of my pussy like an erupting volcano.

Sam thrust into me and held it there, every muscle in his body tense. We came together and didn't let go of one another until our bodies told us we could relax.

Sam lowered his lips to mine and kissed me gently.

"I think I love you, too," he said. He gazed into my eyes. "Let's make a deal."

I brushed hair from his forehead and sighed. "Name it."

"You try to be nothing like your father and I'll do the same."

I smiled at him. "You've got yourself a deal. Now shut up and kiss me again."

EPILOG: Allie

Six months later...

If you had ever told me that I would be happy as the wife of a high school football coach in Tipton, Nebraska, I would have called you insane.

After growing up and working in Atlanta, Tipton seemed like a whole other world to me. There were no crowds or traffic jams, no one trying to rob you or jack your car, the air was fresh and clean, and life seemed to move at a slower pace.

And that was just fine with me.

I wanted my life with Sam to last a very long time, the slower the pace, the better.

* * *

I was sitting on the bleachers on a cool, fall Friday night, watching Sam coach his team to a victory over Somerville High.

I loved watching him work. It was clear that he loved his players and they loved him.

As I watched him, my mind wondered back over everything that had happened over the last few months.

Sam asked me to marry him and I said yes.

He asked if I would give life in Tipton a chance and I said yes.

He offered to coach the small high school team for free and they said yes.

He asked if I would live in the farmhouse he grew up in with his mother until he could have us a house built on the property.

I said yes, if it was okay with his mom.

She said yes.

We were as happy as two people could be.

As I watched Sam on the sidelines, I slipped the handkerchief I'd doused with Aramis from my purse and held it to my nose. I took a long whiff.

My water works started to flow.

I couldn't wait to get Sam home.

Aramis smelled wonderful on a handkerchief.

It smelled even better on the neck of the man I loved.

THE END

Don't miss out!

Visit the website below and you can sign up to receive emails whenever Amy Brent publishes a new book. There's no charge and no obligation.

https://books2read.com/r/B-A-GACH-ZNNNB

BOOKS 2 READ

Connecting independent readers to independent writers.

Did you love *Filthy Coach*? Then you should read *Filthy Daddy*[1] by
Amy Brent!

2

***What's a man gotta do when not one, but two disasters hit him in the
face: A will that forces him to marry, and the s*x-on-heels daughter
of his fake wife!***

She's the sunshine I never thought I needed in my life.

A cherry so ready to be plucked.

And I want to be the lucky man.

As her fake dad, I am supposed to protect her, take care of her.

And all I want to do is kiss her like there's no tomorrow,

Touch her like every part of her body belongs to me,

And f*ck her senseless...until she sees those stars screaming my
name and begging for more.

---

1. https://books2read.com/u/38Qy8L

2. https://books2read.com/u/38Qy8L

Well, I've never played by the rules,

And Jessica seems more than eager to call me daddy, as I order her to spread those legs for me.

But I'll need to create this rule in our relationship – it will be our little secret.

We can't let it out and risk our fake arrangement.

Because that will cost me everything I've worked so HARD for.

Turns out Jessica doesn't want to play by the rules too!

And I'll have to choose – between my business, my fake wife and her sweet daughter.

The sweetest decisions are also the toughest.

Jessica baby, Daddy's gonna make you come...back to him...forever.

And all hell breaks loose when I announce my decision to the world!

Also by Amy Brent

Filthy
Filthy Boss
Filthy Doctor
Filthy Professor
Filthy Seal
Filthy Cowboy
Filthy Daddy
Filthy Coach

Forbidded
The Doctor's Fake Marriage

Forbidden
Fake Fiance
One More Chance
Crave Me
My Best Friend's Dad
The Doctor's Fake Marriage
Dad's Best Friend

Forbidden Fantasies
Daddy's Business Partner
Daddy's Friend
Daddy O
Climbing His Corporate Ladder
Taken By Daddy's Boss
Filthy Liar

Standalone
Teachers' Pet
Filthy Box Set
Knocked Up By My Brother's Best Friend
My Best Friend's Brother
My Best Friend's Ex
Say You're Mine
Club Desire Box Set
My Boyfriend's Dad
Fighting For Her
Forbidden Love Box Set
Love Undercover
Friends With Benefits
A Royal Menage
Baby Fever
Vegas Baby
Brother's Best Friend for Christmas
Christmas With My Best Friend's Dad
My Son's Sitter
Single Dad's Christmas Present
Surrendering To 3 Alphas

Because I Love You
Catching Up With Daddy
Claiming Cinderella
Double Trouble
First Love
First Time
Knocked Up By My Brother's Best Friend
My Best Friend's Boyfriend
Pretend Daddy
Redemption
Roomies With Benefits
Royally Yours
Rub Me The Right Way
Show Stopper
That One Night
The Baby Contract
Truth Or Dare
Santa's Naughty List
Quickie on Christmas
Con Man